Perfectly Imperfect

A Dose of Love, Book 2

By

Jill Boyce

Editor: Cynthia Hickey

Book Design by Forget Me Not Romances

This book is a work of fiction. Names, characters, Places, incidents, and dialogues are either products of the author's imagination or used fictitiously. Any resemblance to actual persons, living or dead, or events is coincidental.

ISBN: 978-1-0880-4683-8

Acknowledgments

I praise God, who whispered these stories to my heart and placed the perfect people along my writing path at the perfect time.

I thank my husband, children, father, in-laws, stepmother, family, and friends for their love and support.

I am grateful to my mentor and friend, Carrie Turansky, for her generous spirit and wisdom, and my editor, Cynthia Hickey, for believing in my work.

I especially thank my mother, who passed away six years ago on the day of my daughter's birth. Her death inspired my first book, *Harte Broken*. She instilled in me the love of books and the desire to dream big. I love you, Mom.

My hope is my stories will provide comfort, laughter, and encouragement to my readers. May God bless you all.

There is no fear in love. But perfect love drives out fear, because fear has to do with punishment. The one who fears is not made perfect in love. 1 John 4:18

Chapter 1

"Cleanliness is Next to Godliness"

Ms. Blaire Cunningham
Apartment 42-H, Rose Avenue
New York, New York 10021

June 25, 2019

Dear Ms. Cunningham,

We sincerely appreciate your questions regarding the legitimacy of the cleaning power of our product. Rest assured, Clean-all Wipes have served American households for generations. We stand behind our motto, "We're green, but still keep it clean." That said, yes, the wipes do remove up to 99.99% of germ-causing bacteria and viruses, not limited to, but including MRSA, Strep, Flu, and as you specifically inquired about, the common cold. While there is no recommended number of times to wipe down surfaces, we at Clean-All feel once or twice daily should suffice. As you asked, six times may not be necessary. Sadly, we do not have copies to send to customers of the original "petri dish studies" to prove our product's germ-fighting power. Still, we pledge that our FDA approval is valid. Thank you for reaching out to us, and we hope you have a healthy and germ-free summer!

With best regards,

Melanie Altywer
Clean-All Customer Service

PS. I do not recommend using the wipes on the skin. I would encourage you to continue using your aforementioned "massive pile of hand sanitizer" instead.

Blaire Cunningham plucked a Clean-All antiseptic

wipe from the yellow container and swiped it across her white kitchen countertop. She inhaled, and the bleach tingled her nose— nothing like the scent of a clean space to calm her spirit and ease her fears.

Leaning down, she inspected the countertop. Not a speck in sight, but that didn't mean she'd erased every germ. She grabbed another wipe and repeated the process.

A buzzing sound from within her black work bag pulled her out of her cleaning trance. Who would call her at 6:45 a.m.? She walked to the bag and pulled out her phone, noting the name on the call screen. *Stella Cunningham*. A sigh escaped her lips.

Blaire punched the green button and placed the phone to her ear as she lifted her bag off the floor. "Hello, mother. How are you today?"

"Good morning, Blaire. I'm glad I caught you," her mother passed over pleasantries and dove headfirst into the matter at hand. "I wanted to remind you about the planning meeting for the Gala. I expect you to be there. It's today at 5:00 p.m. Sharp."

Blaire closed her eyes and pinched the bridge of her nose. "Mother, I told you yesterday I can't get there by five...I have a meeting with my Fellowship Director this evening. I can't miss it. It's my end of the year review. This meeting determines if I advance in the program."

Her mother ignored everything Blaire said, did, or wanted. So, it didn't surprise Blaire when Stella Cunningham cut her off with a curt, "I expect you to be there. The Gala is a memorial to your sister. How will it look to the NY Trust Board if you aren't there?"

"I don't know, mother. How will it look? You know, I loved Megan. I want the Gala to succeed." What an understatement. Ever since Blaire lost Megan years ago to meningitis, she'd tried to make up for her sister's absence. To correct the injustice of a horrible disease stealing the most beautiful soul. Staring at a smudge on the wall, Blaire realized her mother had said her name.

"Blaire. Blaire, are you listening to me?"

She was not, but Blaire didn't want to endure another verbal lashing from her mother, so she pretended she'd paid attention. "Of course, mother. I'm listening."

Blaire could almost hear her mother's firm nod through the phone. "Good. There's nothing I despise more than having to repeat myself."

Glancing at the microwave clock, Blaire worried she'd be late to work if she didn't leave soon. "Mother, I hate to cut this short, but--"

Before she could slink away, her mother interrupted, "I don't know why you bother with that silly job. Hospitals--they are filled with germs. You know, Megan planned to devote her life to the family business and its legacy. I do wish you'd try to be more like your sister."

The phone clicked off, and Blaire stared at the blank screen. "Wow, thanks, Mother, for understanding," she spoke to the dead line. "You know Megan's Gala is important to me, and I miss her, too, but perhaps we can reschedule the meeting. What? No problem? You understand and want your sole surviving daughter to be happy? Great! Thanks, Mother. Goodbye."

Blaire dropped the phone into her bag and scanned her all-white and stainless-steel apartment for imperfections. Finding none, she flicked off the light switch, shut the door behind her, and turned her three locks. One lock did not suffice--at least not for Blaire.

Patting her head, Blaire ensured every chestnut-colored hair remained in place in her tight, low ponytail. She scurried down the hallway of her apartment building. She almost ran over her neighbor, Mrs. Leibowitz, heading toward the elevator. *Whew. Perfect timing.* Blaire willed Mrs. Leibowitz to press the dingy, cream-colored elevator buttons for her. Who knew what germs lurked on them?

Mrs. Leibowitz pushed the down button and stepped inside ahead of Blaire.

Blaire followed suit and released another sigh. She scooted to the opposite side of the enclosure, as far away from her fellow passenger as possible. Raising her hand, she gave a slight wave, glancing at her wiry neighbor. "Good morning Mrs. Leibowitz."

The grey-haired woman stood stooped over, her back curved from seventy-plus years of life experience. She clutched a brown leather handbag close to her body and peered at Blaire through squinted, mistrusting eyes. "Good? What's so good about it?" She sneezed, not covering her mouth. "I've got a terrible cold, and it's a terrible day."

Blaire cringed and flung her elbow in front of her face like a vampire with a cape. "I hate to hear that," she muffled through her arm. She remained silent, trying to hold her breath for the rest of the trip downstairs.

As soon as the door opened, Mrs. Leibowitz exited, and a giant exhale escaped Blaire's mouth. *Phew. Was it too early in the day to wipe her face off with the sanitizer tucked in her purse?* She shivered and stepped off the elevator, heading toward the bank of mailboxes.

She surveyed the stack of silver boxes. Blaire pulled another cleaning wipe out from a travel pack in her purse and gave a quick scrub to the front of the box labeled 42-H. *There. All clean with Clean-All. Hey, that'd make a great commercial.* Her mouth formed a half-grin. She opened her mailbox and pulled out a stack of letters and advertisements.

Blaire placed the letters in her purse, but one of the flyers made her pause. Her eyes lingered on the red paper. It boasted scenic views of a lake with billowing trees in the background. Across the top, it read, "Want to make a difference? Join Doctors Working Beyond today. Now filling an open position in Guatemala. Come change lives one visit at a time." *Huh.*

Blaire wanted to change lives…to make a difference like Megan would have wanted…but she also had responsibilities here. Like finishing her residency and making good on a pledge to her big sister.

An older, dark-haired man standing behind her grumbled, startling her.

Still holding the flyer, Blaire peeked over her shoulder and noted a small line forming behind her. Three people behind the man whispered and cast glances her way.

The gentleman blew out an exasperated sigh. "Listen, lady, get a move on it. We all know you've got hang-ups, but can you shelf them for today? I've got an important meeting to get to, and you're making me late."

Locking her mail slot with a brass key, Blaire turned to him. "I'm sorry, sir, but you can't be too careful." She slid out of his way and tossed the wipe in the trash.

Blaire's landlord approached her from the hallway as she pushed the building door open, ready to leave.

"Ms. Cunningham, can I have a minute of your time?"

She paused. "Sure, what can I do for you?"

The burly man bore a few days-worth of stubble on his chubby chin. "I've gotten several complaints around the building over the last few weeks…about your…quirks."

Blaire's brow furrowed. "My quirks? What quirks?"

"Well, like how you scrub other tenants' mailboxes and doorknobs. Or how you kick the elevator buttons instead of touching them. Yesterday, Mrs. Leibowitz rode to the tenth floor because you kicked the wrong button. She was not happy."

Blaire doubted that woman was ever happy, but she pasted a forced smile on her face. "I'm only attempting to keep the building healthy. I'll try to be less quirky, though."

He stared at her for a second and then gave her a nod. "See that you do."

Spinning on her heel, Blaire shoved the front door open and readied herself to face the day. As she walked onto the city street, a tall man with jet-black hair and a dark suit blew past.

He kept his head down, oblivious to her proximity. The man grazed her as he dashed by, crushing her pinky toe.

"Ouch!" Blaire shouted, hopping up and down on one foot, trying to shake the throbbing from her injured toe.

The man acted like he hadn't heard her and continued down the street, unaware of the pain he'd inflicted upon her.

"Thanks a lot," she called to his retreating, broad-shouldered back. Blaire slipped off her red pump, which boasted the only color in her otherwise black and white ensemble. After ensuring no bones were broken, she replaced her shoe. If she didn't have the end of the day review later, she would've started her day in scrubs and plastic clogs, but she planned to change into scrubs for work and then have her interview attire ready.

Blaire hobbled down the street, her pinky toe pulsating. Stopping at the next intersection, she waited for the "Walk Now" light to appear.

Suddenly, Blaire noticed the familiar dark suit responsible for her maimed foot standing beside her. She started to tell him to be more careful and watch where he was going, but the man took a step into the street. Shifting her gaze, she saw a massive bus barreling toward the man.

Gasping, Blaire lunged forward, and grabbed the man, yanking him back to safety. In the process, Blaire lost her balance. She toppled over, pulling him down with her, and the mystery man landed on top of her.

"Oof," was all Blaire uttered. How can someone be so obtuse? He could've died. Slowly opening her eyes, she met the stranger's gaze. His chiseled jaw and tanned skin caught her by surprise.

He scrunched his forehead, concern clouding his eyes. "Are you okay?"

Blaire's pulse quickened, and she struggled to respond. Was she okay? She wiggled her toes and fingers, and aside from her pinky toe still smarting, everything else was intact. "I-I think so. Except I can't breathe," she squeaked.

The man's ebony eyes searched her face. "Oh, no. What can I do?"

Blaire spoke with short breaths, "You could get off me. I think that might be the problem."

A relieved smile spread across his face, revealing knee-weakening dimples. He put his hands on the ground, ready to push away from Blaire, but paused. "Are you sure you're okay otherwise?"

Drawing in a shallow breath, Blaire noted his cologne carried a masculine scent of sandalwood and spice. "Yeah, I'm fine. Except for my toe you crushed earlier."

He lifted himself from the ground and extended a hand to her, helping her up, too. "I'm sorry…I didn't realize. I've been distracted today. I'm late for an important meeting at the NY Trust, and, well, it's no excuse…I guess you can't control everything…nothing is perfect." He ran a hand through his ebony hair. "Hey, you saved my life. Thank you."

Her face warmed, and she shifted her eyes to the ground, avoiding his compliment. No one is perfect. No one uttered those words in the Cunningham household, no sir. Phrases like, "Winners never quit," and, "We expect the best, nothing less," were tossed around her home. If it hadn't been for Megan, Blaire didn't think she'd have survived her pressure-cooker childhood.

"Well, I'm glad I could help. I've got to run, or I'll be late to work. Are you sure you're okay?"

The gentleman's eyes lingered on her face a few seconds longer before he waved away her concern. "No, I'm fine. You have a good day, Miss." He took her hand in his.

Buoyed with adrenaline from her unexpected heroism intermixed with the jolt from the handsome stranger, Blaire's hand trembled at his touch. "You, too." Blaire sent him a smile before whizzing away.

On the way to work, she stopped for coffee and scanned her outfit for imperfections after her tumble. Finding none, she turned her attention to the familiar barista. Blaire peeked at her watch. 7:30 a.m. At least her favorite coffee cart, usually the cleanest one in the city, stood one block from her job as an infectious disease first-year fellow at New York Memorial.

The barista waved and sent Blaire a welcoming grin and Blaire gave her order to the girl; tall mocha latte. Always the same.

The girl handed the to-go cup to Blaire, who accepted it after giving it a thorough rub down with her umpteenth wipe of the day.

The barista shook her head and swiped at the counter with a worn, damp towel.

The action sent shivers down Blaire's spine. "Thanks!" She gave the girl a nod as she hurried down the block to start her final shift in the intensive care unit.

Chapter 2

"Nothing Ventured, Nothing Gained"

Felipe Martinez
425 Belle Calle
Santiago del Alma, Guatemala

June 20, 2019

Mr. Martinez,

We hope this letter finds you well. I regret to inform you since Doctors Working Beyond will no longer provide La Clinica with volunteer medical providers, the city council voted to close the clinic. Without consistent supervisory staff available consistently, we cannot allow it to remain open. Also, the city council needs the building for other endeavors. Please know we appreciate all you have done for our community.

Best Regards,

Julio Blando, Mayor of Santiago del Alma

Felipe Martinez stared at the letter from the town Mayor

he'd carried in his suit coat pocket with him from Guatemala. Standing on the sidewalk in New York City after a stunning dark-haired woman saved him from being plowed down by a bus, he struggled to focus. After her heroic effort resulted in an unexpected, but not unpleasant fall, he couldn't stop thinking about her beautiful face. Well, that and about almost becoming a human pancake on the city street.

He shook his head and crumpled the paper into a ball, tossing it in the nearest waste bin. He couldn't get distracted today. His meeting with the NY Trust, who oversaw Doctors Working Beyond, was in ten minutes, and he couldn't be late.

He recalled his conversation with Juanita from earlier in the week. Sixty-five-year-old Juanita Alvarez, the clinic's devoted and only nurse, had shuffled into the room. "Yes, how can I help?"

"I'm going to New York to see if I can convince the NY Trust to continue sending clinical volunteers. Can you cover things at the clinic while I'm gone? I know we can't continue visits, but you can schedule future appointments and field questions. Maybe follow up on blood pressure and sugar checks."

The older, grandmotherly woman nodded her head. "Not a problem."

Felipe sighed. "Thanks, Juanita, the city is giving us six weeks to find a permanent physician for the clinic."

Juanita nodded her head, her mouth set in a firm line. "Think you can find someone?"

"I have to...no other choice." He said a silent prayer for God to provide a solution.

Juanita placed a comforting hand on his shoulder. "I know how much the clinic means to you. I'm proud of what you've built for the community...and your parents would be proud of you, too."

Felipe had known Juanita since childhood. He'd attended college in Southern California, paying his way through school by working as a medic at night. Juanita often sent him small sums of money or trinkets in care packages. His dream was to go to medical school after college. Instead, he returned home to Santiago del Alma during his senior year to care for his community. Or what was left of it.

Juanita clucked her tongue. "You look so serious. What's going on in that head of yours?"

Sending his beloved friend and colleague a half-smile, he shook his head. "Nothing. I guess I can't believe everything that happened. So many lives lost. I thought we were making a difference with the clinic."

Shifting her weight, Juanita took a moment before opening her mouth. "You know...those people that died...it wasn't your fault. Beating yourself up about it won't bring them back. Not a single one. You need to accept God's grace and forgiveness."

Maybe Juanita was right. "I'll try." Deep down, though, he knew he should have been here when it happened. He might have been able to do something. He'd heard of survivor's guilt...but the weight on his shoulders seemed like more than that. Ever since the day Juanita called him about the tragedy, his life had turned upside down. He didn't think it would ever be the same again.

Chapter 3

"If It's Not Broke, Don't Fix It."

Arriving at work, the intensive care unit was full. Blaire flew from patient to patient in a frenzy. She'd taken time to inhale a granola bar, a fruit cup, and another round of coffee before tackling the rest of her patient list. She found comfort in pre-packaged food as it held less risk for food-borne illnesses.

After compiling her notes for the day's final rounds, she entered the last patient's room on her list. The man laid in bed with a large, oozing wound on his lower leg. A wound vacuum attached helped drain the infection and keep the area sterile. She'd changed the dressing, a job she wasn't fond of, but barreled through with only moderate flinching.

As she finished, the patient sent her a guarded look and tossed her an insincere, "Thanks."

Blaire walked to the door and removed her PPE, short for

Personal Protective Equipment, or as she thought of it, "the only way she was making it through the day." She threw the gown, gloves, and mask in the trash. *Ah.* On to her favorite part; handwashing. She scoured her hands with soap and water hot enough to boil a lobster.

Exiting the patient's room, she turned. "I'm all done here. Do you want the light on or off?"

The patient watched her process and frowned. "Light off, please."

After a final pump from the hand sanitizer station, Blaire's shoulders relaxed.

As she headed down the hall to join evening rounds, Blaire bumped into her Chief Fellow and ex-boyfriend, Darren Byrne. At thirty-one years of age, he walked with the confidence obtained from tackling several fellowship years with prowess.

He ran a hand through his wavy, brown hair as he approached Blaire.

She sent him a smile, which he did not return.

His mouth settled in a straight line, and he uttered a brief, "Hey."

Furrowing her brow, Blaire matched his level of enthusiasm with her tone and said, "Hey. Is something wrong?"

He stared at the floor and only the rhythmic beeping of a nearby monitor broke the silence. After several seconds, he raised his head to meet her gaze. "Uh, yeah. Dr. Sedgewick wants to meet with you now."

She peered at her crumpled scrubs and wondered if she had time to change into her road-rashed, but less mussed, black and white suit. "Right now?" she asked, raising a brow.

He remained serious and gave a curt nod. "Yeah, right now."

A wave of dread washed over Blaire, and her chest tightened. "Any idea what this is about?"

Refusing to meet her eyes, Darren rubbed the back of his neck with one hand and looked away. "He didn't say, but he wants me to come, too."

"Okay, well, we might as well get this over with." Blaire's stomach tensed, and her palms began to sweat. She followed Darren down the hallway to the elevator and took the short ride to the administrative floor. Why did the director need her at this instant? And with Darren?

Arriving at Dr. Sedgewick's door, Blaire took a deep breath. She gave a quick rap on the door and waited.

A gruff, "Come in," bellowed from the other side of the closed door.

Blaire opened the door and found her intimidating, salt-and-pepper haired boss, Dr. Michael Sedgewick. He'd held the status of Program Director of the Infectious Disease Fellowship at New York Memorial for a million years. Blaire dared not speculate on the man's age. "Sir, you wanted to see me?"

He turned his attention away from a stack of papers and his laptop, reaching for his coffee cup. Taking a slow sip, he delayed his response for a few seconds. Finally, after scanning a document in front of him, he lifted his eyes to Blaire's. "Yes. Dr. Cunningham, please have a seat. You, too, Dr. Byrne."

Dr. Sedgewick gestured to two brown tufted leather chairs in front of his mahogany desk riddled with stacks of papers.

She glanced to the right and noted her boss's many degrees, awards, and accomplishments framed on the wall. His title boasted more letters following his name than anyone else in the hospital. Sitting before him reminded Blaire of being called to the principal's office in ninth grade for punching a boy who made fun of her meticulous cleaning habits. Blaire swallowed hard.

"Now, then." Her boss folded his hands into a steeple and rested his plump chin on the tips of his fingers. "I have some bad news."

Blaire's stomach plummeted to her feet. "Bad news?"

He nodded. "Yes, unfortunately. You see, I have some…concerns."

She raised her eyebrows. "What kind of concerns? I'm never

late, I'm thorough, and I'm probably the most hygienic physician in the hospital, and that's important in infectious disease."

He gave a slow nod, his fingers still poised below his chin. "Yes, well, that's part of the problem."

Blaire shifted in her seat. "What do you mean?"

Her boss lifted his chin and reached for a stack of papers on his desk. "These are complaints from staff and patients about your behavior."

"My behavior? It must be a mistake." She turned to Darren for support, but he refused to look at her. Blaire returned her attention to her boss, and her cheeks warmed.

"Let's see…ah, yes. Dr. Smith, your attending, stated you fell behind the group during rounds. Daily. He states you went missing on multiple occasions because you took ten minutes at each patient's room to wash your hands."

Blaire raised her hand to interject, "If I may, handwashing is crucial to preventing the spread of germs."

Her boss continued, "Yes, yes, it is. However, I think ten minutes may be too long. If my math is correct, and rounds include twenty patients on average, that would be two hundred minutes devoted solely to handwashing. It's excessive."

Leaning back in her seat, Blaire scrunched her brow. Sweat beaded around the back of her neck. She hadn't been this nervous since her mother took her prom dress shopping and then criticized every facet of each dress Blaire tried on during the five-hour shopping nightmare. *This meeting is what torture feels like.* Dr. Sedgewick *must have studied with Stella Cunningham on how to make a person feel two inches tall.* "What else?"

Dr. Sedgewick picked up another paper from the stack and placed it in front of him. "Here. I just received this one. It's from a patient you saw today. The patient states you kept him from his nap because it took you twenty minutes to…I believe he says," he peered closer at the form, "ah, yes, 'decontaminate'." He looked at Blaire, waiting for her rebuttal.

She wrung her hands in her lap. "Well, okay, yes, that did happen. But it wasn't that bad. It's an exaggeration. You can't fault me for wanting to do things perfectly."

He placed the paperback in its position on top of the stack of grievances. "I see. Dr. Cunningham, I'm worried you won't handle the...more unpredictable aspects of this job. There is an international rural rotation requirement during the second year of training, and I don't believe you will survive it." He paused for a beat before continuing, "I hate to do it, but I have to give you this. He picked up a single sheet and passed it to her.

New York Memorial Hospital
Infectious Disease Fellowship Program, Dr. Michael
Sedgewick, Program Director
225 First Avenue, Suite 3
New York, NY 10016

Dr. Cunningham,
I regret to inform you that the Infectious Disease and Immunology Fellowship Program will not be extending an offer to you for continuation in the program. Effective June 30th, your employment as a fellow will be null and void. Thank you for your efforts over the past year, and I wish you all the best in your future endeavors.

Sincerely,

Dr. Michael Sedgewick

Blaire's mouth fell open. "Wha-what does this mean? You're firing me?" she sputtered.

Dr. Sedgewick returned his focus to his laptop screen as if he'd handed her a two-for-one coupon at the local grocery mart. After a few clicks, he faced her again. "Think of it as a non-renewal of your contract. I'm sorry to bear unpleasant news, but I have to go. I'm covering evening rounds, and I still have several messages to respond to before then. Dr. Byrne can take it from here. He'll recover your identification badge and any other hospital-owned materials." With this final statement, he shuffled through another massive stack of papers and dismissed her.

Stunned, she sat for a second before rising from her chair. Blaire walked to the doorway, her knees shaking.

Once in the hallway, Darren turned to Blaire, staring for a moment before shaking his head. He opened his mouth to speak, but then closed it. After this brief hesitation, he started again, "Blaire...I."

"Did you know this was coming?"

He looked away. "I didn't know for certain..."

Blaire's eyes widened. "Why didn't you say something? I know we aren't together any longer...and I'm...different...but I'm a good doctor. I take great care of my patients."

He frowned. "You do...but working in a hospital, especially in infectious disease...well, it requires one not to maintain a high degree of fear of germs. You are not a great fit in that regard."

In the past, Darren's British accent made her stomach flip with excitement. Today, it sounded critical, and not a little bit know-it-all like the headmaster at school reprimanding her. *Grr.*

"Well, thanks for the heads up," Blaire said, her voice dripping with sarcasm. "I guess I'll leave."

"Wait."

Blinking hard, she tried not to let the pools of tears forming spill over. *What else could he possibly have to say?* "What?"

Darren, looking far more regal than anyone should in rumpled blue scrubs, shifted his weight. "I need your identification badge and locker key."

Blaire's jaw dropped. *Unbelievable.* She closed her eyes, gathering her thoughts before saying something she might later regret. "Fine. That's fine." Blaire yanked her identification badge

17

off her neck and dug her locker key out of her pocket, thrusting the items in her ex-chief and ex-boyfriend's hands.

She stood, staring at Darren for a moment and drew in a deep breath. The scent of bleach, a reminder of the hospital and often a comfort to Blaire, only brought a fresh wave of nausea now. She spun on her heel and marched down the hall. She would not give him the satisfaction of seeing her cry. Or vomit.

Tears filled her eyes as Blaire dashed to the elevator and punched the button with her elbow. She rode down to her workstation housing her bag, grabbed it, and tore out of the hospital.

Chapter 4

"Mother Knows Best"

Once on the city streets, she peered at her watch. 5:30 pm. Great. She'd missed the meeting for Megan's Gala in favor of getting fired. Mother would love that. She reached into her bag and pulled out her phone, punching numbers into the screen with ferocity.

"Hello, Cunningham residence, Edna speaking."

Hearing the unfamiliar voice on the other end of the line came as no surprise to Blaire. Her mother went through maids, chauffeurs, and cooks as often as some people changed clothes. "Edna, this is Blaire Cunningham." A long pause followed her response, and for a moment, Blaire thought she had been disconnected. She pulled the phone away from her ear and saw that the time clock still ran, ticking away the painful seconds of this sparsely worded call with the newest Cunningham staff member.

Placing the phone to her ear again, she cleared her throat. "Hello?"

The mystery woman spoke in a professional, distant tone, with no recognition in her voice. "Yes, I'm here. How may I help you?"

"I'm Blaire."

"Yes, you said that."

"Blaire, as in Blaire Cunningham, the daughter of Anthony and Stella Cunningham."

She could hear some understanding come into Edna's voice. "Oh, Blaire, my apologies. I knew the Cunningham's had a daughter, but I didn't know your name."

Blaire's jaw dropped. Her parents hadn't bothered to tell their newest staff member their daughter's name. *What a cherry on top of a spectacular day.* "Yes, well. It's me. Now, I wondered if I might speak with my mother?"

Edna stalled before speaking again, "Mrs. Cunningham is out on the veranda, wrapping up an important meeting. I'm sure you know Mrs. Cunningham doesn't like to be disturbed during her gatherings. However, you are her daughter…so, just a moment."

Blaire waited through silence, reflecting on the odd, yet not unexpected interchange. Her parents held pivotal business and social positions as part of the Upper East Side echelon. Blaire's childhood consisted of a smattering of staff who handled all the luncheons, cotillions, and private schools. Being raised by many nannies and living in her sister's golden shadow left Blaire well below her parent's high expectations. She sighed.

"Ahem. Good afternoon, Stella Cunningham speaking," her mother spoke in a clipped manner.

Blaire's palms began to sweat. Her mother always had this effect on her. "Hi, Mother."

With a warning tone, her mother rebutted, "Blaire."

"I-I-I'm sorry I didn't make it in time for the meeting.

Her mother made a displeased hum, followed by, "Yes, well. We all make choices, don't we? They aren't all good ones, but that is neither here nor there. Now, I'm finishing up my meeting and getting ready to have dinner with Bitzy and Vida. Is there anything else?"

She shook her head. Her mother's friends always had names that reminded her of a small animal or a beverage. "I wanted…no, I needed to tell you something."

"Well, what is it?" she said.

Blaire could almost hear her mother tapping her foot on the other end of the line. She glanced around the street, searching for a way to tell her mother that she lost her job. A man tossed his half-full coffee cup on the ground, splashing her with the residual contents. She gasped. *Perfect.* "Well, uh, today I got some difficult news at work."

"Oh, that job. Infectious disease. It's beneath you. Now, plastic surgery… that's what you should be doing. Or marry a plastic surgeon. Then, you could stay home and participate in the Benefits. Philanthropy would be much more becoming on you than infectious disease."

Blaire rolled her eyes. Her mother would love it if she married "well" and spent her days raising money for charities at galas and big-wig events. She couldn't imagine the number of disinfectant wipes required to attend such gatherings. Blaire shuddered. "Thanks, mother. No, what I wanted to tell you is my contract was not renewed for the next year at the hospital." She held her breath.

"You got fired?" her mother sounded smug but then lowered her voice to a hushed whisper, "You got fired." She must have realized her guests were only a few feet away in the next room and might hear. Her mother couldn't bear the shame of an offspring failing, even if it was at a job that she found displeasing.

At least Megan, Blaire's older sister, never let her parent's down. "Well, when you put it that way, I suppose, yes, I did."

"Blaire, I don't know what to tell you. Another failure. Although, I suppose this opens the door for the plastic surgeon husband. I can't discuss this problem right now. I have guests, and I need to go attend to them. We can discuss this matter further at a later date."

Blaire hung her head, and warmth filled her cheeks from embarrassment and shame. Her throat tightened. "Mother, I—"

She didn't get to finish discussing her shortcomings with her mother because Stella Cunningham had already ended the call. Without so much as a goodbye. Typical. Blaire moved the phone away from her ear and stared at the black screen for two seconds before bursting into tears.

Chapter 5

"You Can't Always Get What You Want"

Trying to get home as soon as possible, Blaire hopped on a subway--a trial on a typical day. Today presented an added challenge because a disheveled, odorous man sat right next to her and proceeded to cough an unidentifiable green goo all over her side. Convinced she might contract pseudomonas, she held her breath as if she was playing the tunnel game on a long car ride.

As she considered jumping off the moving subway, her stop arrived. As the doors opened, she burst through them and exhaled with such force, another fellow passenger stopped and stared. She leaned over, placing her hands on both knees, trying to catch her breath. At least she had adequate lung capacity. While hunched over and distracted, a tall man who'd she noticed on the subway whizzed past her, grabbing her purse.

It took her a second to realize he was fleeing with her bag and all its precious contents, including her wipes and hand sanitizer. And she needed those once off the subway to decontaminate herself. With no money, credit cards, or identification, she panicked. What would she do now? She sighed, recalling she'd placed her phone in her pants' back pocket after talking with her mother. She reached for it and felt the glorious texture of cold metal. Time to call in reinforcements; her best friends.

"Hello, Mabel Smythe, Esquire speaking."

"Ma-Mabel." Blaire sobbed in between syllables.

"Blaire? Is that you? What's going on?"

Blaire sniffled and drew in a shuddering breath. "I—I got fired and mugged."

Mabel spoke in even, practiced tones of an up and coming young attorney, "What do you mean you got fired and mugged? Calm down. Take a breath. Are you okay?"

"I mean, I got fired and mugged! And on top of that, Darren was there for the firing. It was so humiliating. And yes, I'm okay."

As the youngest Assistant District Attorney of Manhattan at twenty-nine, Mabel had a no-nonsense, take-no-prisoners attitude to all of life. She jumped into her cross-examination of her best friend. "Where are you right now? What are you doing?"

Blaire imagined her friend standing with a briefcase in hand, black stiletto heels on her feet, ready to wave a cab as she interrogated her. Mabel was the world's best multitasker. "I'm standing on a street pondering the point of my existence."

In an even tone, Mabel responded, "Don't be dramatic. You will be ok. Now, I want you to head back to your apartment right now. I finished my work at the office and was on my way home to review some case files, but I'm headed your way. I'll meet you there."

Blaire used the back of her hand to wipe away the puddle of tears on her cheeks. She took a breath and exhaled. "O-ok. Can you call Tiffany?"

"I'll take care of it. Now, you go home and wait for me. We will figure this out together. And don't worry about Darren. Tiffany and

I thought he was a stuck-up snob. You can do better."

Blaire nodded her head, unsure if she agreed. When Mabel gave directions, she expected them to be followed. "Alright. I'll see you soon. Thanks, Mabel."

"See you soon." With that final word, the phone went silent.

Blaire placed her phone in her back pocket and took a few steps down the sidewalk. She paused, recalling her recent purchase of a new floor mop system. When the world fell apart, Blaire sought comfort in one of the few consistencies of life; cleaning.

Hurrying, Blaire hoped to get to her apartment before her friends arrived and give the floors a quick wipe-down. And take a shower. Those thoughts brought a small smile to her face. With a nod of her head, she took off again, with more hope in her steps this time.

Chapter 6

"The Writing's on The Wall"

Livingston Real Estate, LLC.

Ms. Blaire Cunningham
Apartment 42-H, Rose Avenue
New York, New York 10021

June 28, 2019
Ms. Cunningham,

We regret to inform you that this will serve as notice of your impending eviction. You are ordered to vacate the premises aforementioned in the address above within five (5) business days of delivery of this notice to you. Your lease was terminated as you repeatedly violated the POA and Homeowner's Contract Agreement. You disturb the building and its other tenants. Therefore, as an unfit tenant, you are being removed from the building. If you fail to vacate the building by the end of this period, court proceedings will take place to evict you. Thank you for your attention to this matter.

Respectfully,

Robert Livingston, Owner
Livingston Real Estate, LLC.

Blaire stood in front of her apartment door, staring in disbelief at the paper attached to it. She couldn't believe it. *An unfit tenant. Ha!* She bent over backward for these people. True, she knew her neighbors didn't love it when she wiped down everyone's doorknobs and mailboxes…and she did request her landlord check on her apartment from time to time to ensure it met the city code. Who didn't have the dishwasher and disposal checked along with the fire alarms on at least a monthly basis? That was responsible homeownership.

Of course, there was the time she called an emergency tenant meeting because the building installed low-pressure, water-saving showerheads…but honestly, who could take a respectable shower that way? One couldn't be expected to get clean under a light mist.

She yanked the notice from the door and crumpled it in her hands. Blaire found herself so upset she nearly opened the door with her bare hand. She shuddered. Close call.

She tucked her hand inside her shirt, turning it into a makeshift glove, and twisted the knob. It didn't budge. No! Her bag! She smacked her forehead with the back of her other hand in frustration, afraid to touch her face with the front of it.

After a brief debate of whether to sink to the floor in a puddle of tears or scream, she recalled taping an extra key to the underside of her doormat for emergencies at Mabel's behest. She didn't love having it there, and she worried it posed a security risk, but today she was thankful for it. As she couldn't expect much nurturing from her mother, she was grateful for her friends.

She bent down and picked up the edge of the mat with the tips of her fingernails, trying to avoid touching as much filth and ground as possible. Sticking her tongue out in disgust, she peeled the tape off the key and dropped the mat like a hot biscuit fresh out of the oven. Blaire rose and shoved the universal key in the three locks. Hearing the glorious clicks, she sighed with relief. She was home.

Blaire ran for the shower and scoured her body until the hot water ran cold. Stepping out of the shower and placing a white, fluffy towel around her, she noted her arms and legs looked beet red from her decontamination efforts. She smiled and gave herself a nod in the mirror. *Better.*

Combing out her wet hair, Blaire reflected on the events of the day--she had lost her job, her purse, and her home. She didn't know where to go next, but she supposed it had to be up because this must be rock bottom.

She stepped into her bedroom, which was attached to the bathroom, and tossed on a pair of Lululemon black leggings and a grey short sleeve flowy crew-neck t-shirt. Slipping into her furry black slippers, she shuffled her way into the kitchen to make a much-needed caffeine infusion.

Placing the filter and coffee grounds in the machine, Blaire pushed the start button. Why couldn't all of life be as simple as a coffee maker and follow stepwise, methodical rules that resulted in a desirable result--coffee.

As the dark roast brewed, the rich, robust scent filled her apartment and gave her comfort. Now that she was disinfected and nearly caffeinated, she decided to do the next thing that would make her feel better—clean. She pulled out her bucket, myriad of cleaning solutions and sprays, rags, and gloves, along with a surgical mask and goggles. With her full armament on, she went to work.

Forty-five minutes later, with Nikolai Rimsky-Korsakov's *Flight of the Bumblebee* playing at a loud decibel in the background, Blaire heard persistent knocking at her door. She paused from her task of scouring her white countertop, which had reached gleaming status about ten minutes ago. Blaire lifted her eyes to the source of the pounding and met the gaze of her two best friends, Mable and Tiffany. *This probably looked bad.* She wore a bouffant headcover, a blue surgical mask, and a white hazmat suit she'd acquired through less-than-scrupulous methods a year ago from a friend in the microbiology lab.

Both of her friends stood just inside her doorway with their mouths hanging open, and their eyes widened. Blaire forgot she had given Mabel a key to her apartment to keep for emergency use only. She shrugged, supposing this might indeed qualify as an emergency.

"Oh, dear." Tiffany placed a slender hand to cover her mouth. Tiffany Beckwith, a Grove Elementary School teacher, stood at five foot ten inches and had shiny, long blond hair. Her aqua blue eyes only added to her All-American good looks. During summer break, she taught fitness classes at the Apple City Gym. She must have come from the gym as she wore athletic leggings, a zip-up jacket, and cross-trainers.

Tiffany dropped her hand and stepped closer to her friend. "Hi, Blaire. Um, whatcha doing?"

Mabel, wearing a crisp, starched, well-tailored, charcoal grey skirt and matching jacket, with black stiletto heels, stepped forward, interjecting, "What's it look like?" She turned to Tiffany, a hand on her hip. "She's having an early mid-life crisis." Returning her focus to her friend, she spun toward Blaire. "Aren't you?" Mabel placed her briefcase on the floor. She stood and crossed her arms in front of her chest.

Blaire stood straighter and pulled the surgical cap off her head. She started to defend her actions, muffling through her mask, "Fanks a lop, fanks fa da vope ob confidence."

Mabel furrowed her brow. "I couldn't hear a word you said. Take that ridiculous thing off."

Blaire took off her gloves, placing them inside out in the empty cleaning bucket on the floor. Removing the elastic straps from behind each ear, she tossed the mask in the trash can below the countertop. She stripped off her hat, unzipped the white beekeeper's suit, and stepped out of it. A quick squirt of hand sanitizer sitting by her sink completed her ritual, and then she brushed herself off and grinned at her friend. "I said, Thanks a lot, thanks for the vote of confidence."

"Hmfp." Mabel moved toward the white sofa in the tiny living room and took her seat on one end, not waiting for an invitation. She embodied self-assurance. Her dark shoulder-length hair, styled in a blunt bob, contributed to her lawyer look. She looked up at Tiffany and Blaire and raised her brow. "Well, what are you waiting for? Sit down. We need to brainstorm."

Tiffany took a seat in an oversized grey tufted armchair opposite the couch.

Sinking into the other end of the sofa to face the firing squad, Blaire folded her hands in her lap. She raised her head, and before she could utter a single word, fresh tears filled her eyes. "Today was horrible. Truly awful. Everything bad that could happen did."

Mabel relaxed her shoulders, softening a little. She scooted closer to her friend and placed a hand on Blaire's forearm. "Ok, start at the beginning and tell us everything."

Through racking sobs, Blaire sputtered out her story. She told her friends about saving the handsome stranger from becoming roadkill, getting fired from her job at NYU, and then being robbed outside the subway station. Oh, and the eviction notice.

Nodding her head in understanding, Mabel sent her a dose of empathy before resuming her direct attorney persona again. "Well, that does sound bad, but there's nothing to be done about it now. You can only look forward to the future. Which is why I brought you this." She clicked open her briefcase, which she had carried over to the sofa when she sat down. Lifting the lid, Mabel pulled out a red flyer like the one Blaire had found in her mailbox earlier in the day. Mabel sat it on the Lucite coffee table in front of Blaire.

Wiping a tear away from her cheek, Blaire sniffled. She glanced at the paper, trying to understand what she was reading.

La Clinica de Santiago del Alma

Want to Make a Difference in the World?
Have Medical Experience?
Looking for adventure and a fresh start?
Ready to Dive In?

Then, consider joining the medical team at La Clinica in Santiago del Alma, a small town in rural Guatemala with friendly people in need of medical care. Although the clinic needs a long-term provider, any time devoted is appreciated and needed. The only requirements are a willing heart and a valid medical license. Looking for someone to start immediately. Please email felipemartinez12@clinic.med.net for more information.

After scanning the flyer, Blaire lifted her head. Her eyes landed on Mabel's. "I had this same flyer in my mailbox earlier today. What is this? A medical mission trip?"

Mabel gave a nod. "Exactly. It's the perfect opportunity for you. After you told me the hospital wasn't renewing your contract, I remembered seeing this hanging on a board in the coffee shop around the corner from the ADA office. I'd seen the same flyer a few other places in town, so the image stuck. I stopped by the café on my way over here and grabbed one for you."

"But why? Why would I go to Guatemala? Can you even imagine me working there? Do they have limitless hand sanitizer and bleach wipes?"

Tiffany spoke up, "Blaire. This may be the thing you need."

Blaire turned her attention to her soft-spoken friend.

"Think about it. This is a chance to go on an adventure and try something new; to get out of your comfort zone of cleaning chemicals and sterilized spaces. I bet they have fresh air and open skies there. Plus, think of all the good you could do. You are a great doctor, despite your...quirks." She gave a sharp nod toward the rumpled hazmat suit lying on the floor near the counter. "You could help a lot of people."

"I don't know...I don't know anything about rural medicine. That was one of the things in my last review the infectious disease program was concerned about. They questioned if I could handle the international medicine rotation requirement to complete the fellowship. I believe they said, 'The rotation may pose a challenge to the candidate given its unexpected, outside-of-the-box nature.' They basically said that my perfectionism couldn't handle the messier, less predictable aspects of the job...and maybe they were right."

Mabel shook her head with force. "Absolute nonsense. I'm not hearing any of it. You are a smart girl, and if you set your mind to something, I believe you can do anything. That mother of yours did a number on you. And what do the program director and that ex-boyfriend of yours know? So, you like to clean...a lot. I'd rather have a clean doctor than a dirty one any day."

Blaire cracked a grin and gave a small chuckle. "That's true. I guess it wouldn't hurt to send an email to the clinic director and find out more information, like when I'd have to start and what to expect." She put both hands up to caution her friend from getting too carried away. "Not that I'm saying I'll do it, but I'll find out more."

Tiffany clapped her hands together in glee. "Yay! Oh, just imagine, Blaire, this time next week you could be sitting by a lake, basking in the hot sun on an adventure! Ooh, maybe you'll meet a tall, dark, handsome man while you're there." She wagged her eyebrows at Blaire.

Rolling her eyes, Blaire sighed. "Fat chance."

Shaking her head and grinning, her fair-headed friend leaned closer. "You never know. This could be the beginning of a fresh start for you."

Mabel jumped on the bandwagon. "She's right, you know. Promise us you'll think about it, ok?"

Closing her eyes, Blaire tried to think back to earlier that morning when her life still made sense. If she was honest with herself, Blaire didn't know if she could do it. Maybe she should stay home and look into a new career...like telemedicine. She couldn't catch an infectious disease from a computer screen—at least Blaire didn't think so.

"I don't know...it sounds like a lot..."

"Didn't you tell me one of the main concerns your program had with you was your ability to handle the international rotations required to graduate?" Mabel raised a single eyebrow.

Blaire grudgingly nodded her head. "Yes."

"And isn't it true that this medical opportunity occurs in a rural, international local?" Mabel was in full-on lawyer mode.

"Yes."

"So, couldn't you assume then, that if you go on this medical trip to Guatemala, then your program director might reconsider your place in the fellowship?" Mabel closed the lid on her briefcase as if she'd already won the argument.

Blaire frowned. "Objection; leading the witness."

A slow smile began to form at the corners of Mabel's mouth, leading into a full-out grin. She chuckled at her friend's well-times joke. "Sustained. Ok, ok. I'll back off...for today. Tiffany and I will leave you alone to mull this all over. Try not to overthink it, though. Besides, you have Megan's Gala in about a month, so you'd have a definite end date—an out. You go and take this adventure and worst case, you come home in a month."

Tiffany reached over and grabbed Blaire's hand. "She's right. You always try to control everything. Some of the best things in life are uncontrollable, messy even. They could even be fun."

Blaire dropped her head in her hands and sighed. Her friends made a point. "I hear you, and I promise to think about it. I'm not saying yes…but I'll consider it. Now, as much as I appreciate you guys coming to my rescue, I'm beat. This feels like the longest day in history. I'm going to take another shower, put on my pajamas, go to bed, and try to forget today ever happened."

Mabel snapped her briefcase closed, stood, and turned to her now-unemployed friend. "Ok, we'll go, but why don't we all meet for coffee in a few days? Say Tuesday around noon?"

Clapping her hands in excitement, Tiffany said, "Ooh, I've wanted to try out that new place that just opened on 42nd; the one that looks like a coffee bean?"

Mabel turned to Tiffany and rolled her eyes. "Do you actually think you're going to get Mrs. Clean to try a new place without her researching its cleanliness rating and online reviews first. It will take her days to complete her investigation before giving the place the Blaire Cunningham Seal of Approval."

Jumping up, Blaire put her hands on her hips. "Hey, that's not fair. I go to new places." Places that have been adequately researched. "But, why don't we go to our usual place—Tom's Coffee House?" She folded her hands together, pleading.

Click-clacking to the door already, Mabel turned and waved. "Fine. We'll meet at Tom's."

Mabel walked to the door, and Tiffany followed her. She leaned in and gave each of her friends a stiff, but well-meaning hug. Physical touch was not her favorite thing, either. "Thanks guys, for coming over and trying to cheer me up. I love you both."

Reaching for Blaire and pulling her into a second forced embrace, Tiffany squeezed her friend tight. "No problem, babe. We've got your back. Hang in there. See you Tuesday." She gave Blaire a palm-open wave, like she was doing jazz hands in a

Broadway production, and slipped out the door.

Mabel started to slide out, too, but paused and found Blaire's gaze one last time. "Promise you'll think about it."

With a heave of her shoulders, Blaire bobbed her head up and down. "I promise. See you soon."

Her sober friend sent her a half-smile and left.

Blaire closed the door behind her two best friends and tapped the frame three times. She secured each lock, turned around to lean against the door, and slid to the floor. "I promise," she whispered.

Chapter 7

"Read Between the Lines"

From: msedgewick@nymh.net
To: blairecunningham7@ny.met.city.net
Dr. Cunningham,

It surprised me to receive your email about your upcoming international medical trip. If you complete a month successfully at the clinic in Guatemala, it would demonstrate your commitment to change. If you do go, please update me on the progress of your trip. I cannot promise a reinstatement within the Infectious Disease Fellowship. Still, it would go a long way to see that you persevered at addressing our previous concerns regarding your ability to function as a physician with your...hygienic tenacity.

Sincerely,

*Dr. Michael Sedgewick, Infectious Disease Fellowship
Program*
New York Memorial Hospital

Staring at the computer screen illuminating her pitch-black bedroom, she rubbed her eyes. *No way.* Blaire reread Dr. Sedgewick's words and couldn't decide whether to squeal with glee or dive under her covers. Her former boss was offering the opportunity to reclaim her fellowship position. Still, it meant she would actually have to go on the trip. Step out of her comfort zone. *Hmm.*

She peeked at the clock on her computer. If Blaire didn't go to sleep soon, she'd be a zombie in the morning. Not that she had anything to do other than pack up her apartment. All of it. She had to move out by Thursday morning, and glancing around the darkened room, her eyes fell upon a few lone brown boxes stacked in the corner. She had a long way to go. Panic rose in her chest, but she took a slow breath and stamped it down.

Blaire started to close the computer and head to bed, but instead, she paused. Pulling the Guatemala flyer out of her desk drawer, she punched the email address into the "To" section of her reply window.

TO: felipemartinez12@clinic.med.net
FROM: blairecunningham7@ny.med.city.net
SUBJECT: La Clinica provider position
To whom it may concern:

*I am writing to express my interest in the clinic
provider position. I realize this is a volunteer position but
wanted more information about the position's requirements*

and expectations. After recently working as an Infectious Disease Fellow at New York Memorial Hospital, I am taking time to explore new professional challenges. Please send me more details about the clinic at your earliest convenience.

Sincerely,
Dr. Blaire Cunningham

PS. Does Santiago del Alma have a local store that stocks an adequate supply of bleach, soap, and hand sanitizer?

Scanning the email before pressing "send," she then took three pumps from the bulk-size hand sanitizer sitting on her desk. Blaire hopped into bed and inhaled the reassuring smell of 62% alcohol before falling into a deep, satisfying sleep.

Chapter 8

"When Life Gives You Lemons…"

Skimming the email again, Felipe released a sigh of relief. He ran a hand through his dark, short wavy hair. Dropping his head, he whispered a quick prayer of thanks to God for providing an answer.

With cautious optimism, he formulated his response. He didn't want to get his hopes up, only to have them later destroyed. In the past, several physicians had inquired about La Clinica, only to later change their minds.

Felipe shook his head. Those who hadn't taken a chance by coming to his beloved town were missing a huge reward. The people of Santiago del Alma had been through a lot over the years—real tragedy—and pulled through as a family might, resulting in a tight knit community full of tenacity and love.

He recalled a conversation with his mother as he was getting ready to leave for America.

She stood at the sink in the kitchen, drying her hands on a tea towel. A light rain drizzled outside, and Felipe watched a single droplet trail its way down the glass pane above the sink before returning to his packing.

"Felipe, I don't think you should go to school so far from home. You're only eighteen—you're still my baby."

Shoving the reminder of his clothes into a duffel bag, Felipe avoided her worried gaze. "Mom, you know it's been my dream to go to college in California. I want to become a physician and save lives."

His mother stepped closer and lifted his chin, forcing him to look into her eyes. "Felipe, don't forget who you are and where you come from. Family, community, love—that's what matters."

He picked up the duffel bag and slung it over his shoulder. "I won't, Mom. I promise. But I have to go. I love you." He walked out the door and didn't look back.

Life experiences and loss had changed him. Now he found himself at the helm of his town's medical clinic, trying to keep it running, albeit on fumes.

He sat in his closet-size office that abutted the internet café next door. The café owner allowed him to use the wifi for free, a kindness Felipe appreciated since the clinic had no funds left for such things. His fingers hovered above the keyboard, poised to formulate a response. He rolled his head, cracking his neck, and started typing.

TO: blairecunningham7@ny.met.city.net
FROM: felipemartinez12@clinic.med.net
SUBJECT: La Clinica physician position

Dr. Cunningham:

It would be a pleasure to have you join the clinic as a physician volunteer for any amount of time you can offer. Ideally, volunteers serve for at least a month, but any time given helps the community. Santiago del Alma is a beautiful rural town of 8,000 population on the southeastern shore of a large lake used for fishing, boating, and even transportation.

The climate is warm and pleasant, although rain showers are not uncommon. Working at the clinic is a rewarding experience as you immerse yourself in local culture and get to know the town's kind people well.

Most of the townspeople do not speak English, and some not even Spanish, as a local Mayan language is common. However, this should not concern you as my long-time assistant and the clinic's nurse, Juanita, speaks all three. She has lived here all her life and knows the patients well.

The clinic operates from 8:00-4:00 p.m. Some days, we close the clinic and travel to a nearby Finca (farm area) to serve more remote areas. Many of these patients would not receive medical care otherwise.

After the clinic closes for the day, you may enjoy many activities. The town offers a few family-run bistros and outdoor activities such as fishing, hiking, and boating abound. The town's beauty is unmatched anywhere else.

I work as the Clinic Director, and the City of Santiago del Alma provides the building space. I have experience as an EMT and can assist with triage, intake, and emergencies.

In closing, I hope you will join us at the clinic. Again, any time you can offer is welcomed. If you have any questions, do not hesitate to let me know. You could join the staff at your earliest convenience, but there aren't funds available for your airfare--I apologize. However, I can pick you up from the airport as the clinic is a bit of a drive from there.

Blessings,
Felipe Martinez
La Clínica de Santiago del Alma Director

PS: They do not have hand sanitizer at the local store, but they carry bleach and plenty of soap.

Chapter 9

"…Make Lemonade"

Blaire opened the door to Tom's Coffee House and inhaled the calming scent of the rich, full-bodied house roast. Reaching into her purse, she retrieved her travel-size hand sanitizer. A flip of the lid, a quick squirt, and an expedient rub of her hands further relaxed Blaire. Ah--clean and safe. She sighed.

She stepped forward to take her place in line to order. Scanning the room, her eyes landed on her two best friends planted at a small table in the far corner of the café. She gave them a wave of recognition and smiled.

Tiffany looked as if she'd just left the gym, wearing black leggings and a breezy pink top. She nodded her head and returned a warm grin to her friend.

Mabel looked less congenial and tapped a finger to the watch on her wrist, letting Blaire know she was in a hurry. She wore grey dress pants, a cream short sleeve blouse, and had her briefcase sitting next to her on the floor.

Blaire glanced down at her own choice of outfit, green scrub pants, and a white t-shirt she got as a promo from ordering a one thousand count box Clean-All Wipes that read 'If you can dream it, we can clean it,' across the front. Not a high point in her life.

Arriving at the front of the line, she turned her attention to the barista. The barista sent Blaire an insincere smile. He wore a black apron and matching hat with different inspirational quotes across the front of both. "Welcome to Tom's Coffee, where we try to make your tomorrow better, today," he said in a flat, dead-pan voice.

Waiting for him to break character and deliver the punchline, Blaire paused before answering. When she realized he was serious, she cleared her throat, "Ahem. Uh, thanks. I think I'll take a caramel macchiato, hot."

He still didn't crack a smile. "Anything else?"

Maybe his week had been worse than hers. "Nope. That's it."

He gave her a nod and turned his attention to the next customer.

She slid down the line and grabbed her drink from the next barista. Even on a Tuesday in the middle of the week, the lunch hour packed the little caffeine hub. Blaire pulled her arms close to her sides, trying to avoid touching fellow coffee-goers. Slinking through the maze of tables, she kicked her seat out with her foot and sat down. Blaire dug through her bag. Retrieving a wipe, she rubbed the entire tabletop surface before lifting her head and acknowledging her friends.

Tiffany sent her a pitying half-smile, while Mabel shot her a grimace and stern shake of the head in disapproval.

Blaire raised her eyebrows. "What? Don't you want the space where you eat and drink to be germ-free?"

Mabel rolled her eyes. She took a drink of her black coffee before responding, "Oh, yes. Please. By all means, save us from invisible agents of filth lying in wait on this table." She gestured with her hand in front of her, palm facing up as if to say, "carry on."

Blaire tossed the soiled wipe in a nearby trash can and crossed her arms in front of her chest. "There. I'm done anyways. Now, I have some important news to tell you both."

Leaning in, Tiffany's eyes lit up. "You're going to go, aren't you?" She took a sip of her herbal green tea.

Swallowing hard, Blaire debated for a few seconds before answering, "Yeah, I'm going to do it. I'm going to Guatemala. It hasn't fully sunk in yet."

Mabel punched her fist in the air. "Yes! I knew it. I knew you'd do it. Good for you. This will be a great change. I'm proud of you…have you told your parents?"

Blaire's hands began to tremble. She shook her head slowly. "No. I can only imagine what my mother will say. Ever since Megan--" her voice broke, and tears filled her eyes. "Well, you guys know I'll never live up to their expectations. I'm a huge disappointment to Stella Cunningham."

Tiffany placed a comforting hand on Blaire's and gave it a squeeze. "We know. What about your apartment? Don't you have to be out by tomorrow?"

Pushing her tears back down, Blaire relaxed her shoulders. "No, thankfully, my landlord agreed to give me an extra day to finish packing. So, I wanted to ask if one or both of you could help me move Thursday because I'm leaving for Guatemala this weekend."

"I can't be there tomorrow to help you until five or six p.m., but I can pick up food and come over to finish up and provide moral support." Mabel threw back the rest of her coffee. She glanced at her watch for the third time. "I've got to run."

Blaire lifted a brow and took a drag from her cup. "Big case today?"

Nodding her head, Mabel tossed her cup and picked up her briefcase. "Yeah, I have a preliminary hearing, and I need to go over a few files beforehand. Will you be mad if I cut out early?"

Shaking her head, Blaire smiled. "Nah, I get it. Go save the world. Or at least New York City. I'll see you tomorrow evening…and thanks, Mabel. For the push. Oh, I almost forgot. Can you come with me Friday night or Saturday to get things for the trip?"

With a quick nod, Mabel agreed. She walked around to Blaire's side of the table and gave her a brief but sincere hug. "You got it. I love you, but I need to run." She waved bye to Tiffany and shot out of the coffee shop.

"I hate to say it, but I need to head out, too." Tiffany sent Blaire a smile and drank the remainder of her herbal tea. "I've got a training session at 1:30 pm and then a group fitness cardio class right afterward." Her aquamarine eyes lit up. "Hey, I have a great idea! You could come with me to the gym. There's nothing better than an endorphin rush from exercise. What do you say?"

The idea of sweating in a room with other people--their germs dripping onto the floor where she would be asked to lay to do stretches--gave her chills. *No, thank you. There weren't enough disinfectant wipes in the entire world.* Instead, she muttered, "Hmm. Well, that's an idea, all right."

Blaire smacked the table with her hand as if inspiration had struck like a lightning bolt. "You know, I'd better go pack. Like I said, I've still got a ton of things to go through, and I don't want all this work to fall upon you tomorrow. You are coming to help me, right?"

Tiffany sent her a broad grin. "Of course, I'll be there. Well, I'm going, but the fitness door is always open."

"Thanks." Blaire placed her cup in the recycling bin and splashed on a final dose of sanitizer. "Want some?" She tilted the bottle to Tiffany.

Tiffany furrowed her brow. "No, thanks. You know, using so much of that stuff cannot be good for you."

"Nonsense. Getting sick, now that's what's not good for me. Ok, suit yourself. I'll see you in the morning at my place…and thanks again, Tiffany. You're the best."

Her friend leaned in and gave her a hug, despite Blaire stiffening in response. "No problem. See you tomorrow."

Blaire waved bye to her friend, who often took the place of a mother in her life. She didn't know what she would do without Tiffany and Mabel. They teased her at times, but they were always there for her. Maybe Mabel was right, and this adventure would be good for her…but that didn't mean she wasn't going to take every cleaning supply she owned with her.

Chapter 10

"A Half-Baked Idea"

Felipe nearly jumped out of his wooden desk chair. Sitting in his minuscule office, he exclaimed, "Woohoo!" as Juanita walked past.

She paused at the open door and put her hands on her hips. "What's so, woohoo?"

He tore his eyes away from his computer screen and grinned at his long-time friend. "Oh, only that I've bought the clinic some time. I got an email from Dr. Blaire Cunningham in New York City, and she's agreed to come for at least the next month. Isn't it great?"

With one hand still planted on her hip, Juanita brushed a silver strand of hair away from her sun-tanned face and smirked. "New York City, huh? You think someone from New York will make it here?"

"Why not? She sounds experienced and knowledgeable. She

doesn't seem fussy, and I think she'll do great. Who knows? Maybe she'll decide to stay." His grin widened, and he locked his fingers behind his head. Satisfied with himself, Felipe leaned back in his chair.

Juanita clucked her tongue. "Ah, I hope it works out. I'll go to church today and pray for you and this clinic…but be careful. I don't want you to be too disappointed if she doesn't stay. We still might have to close, you know—"

Felipe started to interrupt his motherly colleague.

She raised a hand, stopping his interjection. "And if we do, it's not your fault. You cannot blame yourself or continue to feel guilty."

He frowned. "Juanita, you don't know—"

"I do know. I do. I was here when it happened, remember? It was a horrible thing. But you couldn't have saved them. No one could have."

Felipe's shoulders sagged. Juanita's words held truth, but he resisted accepting them. She was wrong. It was his fault. He'd let his family down, and now all he could do to make it right was to keep the clinic open and serve his hometown. "Well, I'm glad she's coming. Right now, that's all that matters. The city won't shut us down for at least another month, and by then, maybe I'll have a plan."

A small smile formed at the corners of Juanita's lips. "Ok, Felipe. If anyone can do it, I believe you can. Now, are you going to sit here all day or are you going to come to help me get things ready for our city slicker guest?"

He clicked the laptop lid closed and stood, stretching his arms wide. "Absolutely. Let's start in the spare room upstairs." He exited the office, flicking the switch off to the single, dusty lightbulb hanging in the center of the room. Following Juanita to prepare for the new physician's arrival, he prayed for God to make Dr. Cunningham fall in love with his beloved town.

Chapter 11

"Only Time Will Tell"

"You're going where?" Stella Cunningham's shrill

voice pierced Blaire's under-caffeinated state. It caused the formation of what promised to become an epic headache.

Blaire paced back and forth in her living room, dodging packed boxes at her feet. "I said I'm going to Guatemala. On a volunteer medical trip. I leave Sunday morning, first thing." She knew her parents would not understand her taking this trip. Still, she had hoped they might be distracted by upcoming social events, so she could slip out of town without creating a commotion.

"Blaire Elizabeth Cunningham, I cannot condone you flitting across the world like this. I'm sure it's unsafe, and besides, how do you expect to manage with your...condition?"

Her face warmed with embarrassment, but she took a deep breath, trying to calm herself. "Mother, I don't have a condition...I simply like things a certain way. Besides, the trip is only a month-long, and I'm sure I can adapt and survive for a month." She doubted if this was true, but based on her mother's reaction, Blaire wasn't going to admit her concerns. She hoped if the trip went well, she might procure her fellowship spot again at New York Memorial.

A gruff voice bellowed through the phone, "Blaire, what's all this about traveling to Mexico?"

Blaire smacked her forehead with her hand. "It's not Mexico, Dad. It's Guatemala. They are two different countries. I'm going to provide care to an underserved community at a volunteer medical clinic. It's a good cause." She prayed this might appeal to his penchant for philanthropy and his affinity for telling his colleagues at the club about his family's high-profile generosity.

"Ahem, I see. Well, I can't say I'm crazy about you traveling by yourself, but it's for a good cause."

Saved by a pounding on her door, Blaire sighed in relief. "A great cause, Dad. I hate to cut our call short, but I think my friend is here. She's going to help me get packed for my trip." She neglected to inform her parents about her current lack of a living situation. Blaire didn't need to hear her mother drone on about how her daughter was now homeless. If Stella Cunningham knew her daughter was going to crash on someone's couch...oh, the horror. "Someone at the club might find out!" she could hear her mother's voice in her head.

"Well, keep us abreast of your trip. You have our number." Anthony Cunningham dismissed her and hung up the phone.

Blaire placed her phone on the table and scurried to her door, turning all the locks, before opening it for her friend.

Tiffany stood in front of her wearing linen shorts, a ratty, older white t-shirt, and tennis shoes, moving attire in place. "So, you're sticking with the three locks, huh?" She tilted her head.

Blaire spun around and reached for an open box in the kitchen, placing plates wrapped in tissue paper and bubble wrap into it. "I'm not having that discussion with you today. We have too much to do, and I already faced the firing squad that is Stella and Anthony

Cunningham."

Taking her shoes off before stepping into the kitchen, Tiffany grabbed another box and joined in the packing. "Ooh, did they stop by? I bet your mom flipped out when she found out you were moving and going on this trip."

Refusing to meet Tiffany's gaze, Blaire picked up a roll of clear packing tape and applied a strip to the box in front of her, pressing it down with force. "Not exactly. I called them and told them about Guatemala, but I didn't say anything about moving. I don't think they could take too much disappointment from their remaining heir in one day."

Tiffany placed a hand on Blaire's arm and paused before speaking, "Oh, Blaire. I'm sorry. I know things with your parents are…hard."

Blaire lifted her head and looked at her friend. "It's fine. Don't worry about it. Today is supposed to be about moving on, right? Change and all that?"

With a quick nod and a smile, Tiffany dropped her hand and returned to her task. "Right. You're absolutely right." She scanned the kitchen and living room to assess what work remained. "It looks like you're almost packed. I got a spot in front of the building, so after we finish with these boxes, we should be ready to load."

"Sounds good. I'll finish this one, and we can take a load downstairs. I'm glad you were able to borrow your parent's SUV. I don't think all this stuff would've fit in a car. Oh, and my landlord let me use his dolly, so we can stack several of these with it. I'd say a few trips should do it."

Ten trips down the elevator and one run-in with a grumpy Mrs. Leibowitz, who uttered a few words Blaire wouldn't repeat followed by "good riddance," and Blaire's apartment stood empty.

Blaire turned in her keys to her landlord, who grumbled an inaudible sentence of farewell. Blaire made it to Tiffany's vehicle before her tears started to flow. She hated change, and lately, that was all life promised her.

Chapter 12

"Ready or Not"

Thursday passed in a blur, and Friday morning, the sun shone through the blinds in Tiffany's living room, announcing the arrival of the "Day of Preparation." Blaire, confused after waking up on her friend's couch, glanced around the room and gathered her thoughts. Today marked the last day of the only life she'd known, a life of perfection. She'd controlled her environment, had unlimited access to cleaning products, and slept on sterilized sheets. Even now, laying on borrowed bedding on Tiffany's couch challenged her sanity.

Blaire rubbed her eyes and realized Tiffany stood dressed and ready for the day in running shorts and a loose t-shirt, coffee mug in hand. "Wow, you're up early. How long have you been standing there?"

Glancing at the digital green numbers on the microwave clock in the kitchen, Tiffany shrugged her shoulders. "Oh, I don't know. Maybe thirty minutes. I tried to let you sleep because today and tomorrow are big days. Are you ready?"

Staring at her friend's optimistic grin, Blaire didn't have the heart to crush her enthusiasm. "I guess." Ready or not. "Give me fifteen minutes to hop in the shower and get dressed, and I'll be good to go. What time is Mabel coming?"

A knock on the door answered Blaire's question. Tiffany called, "Come on in! It's open."

The knob turned, and Mabel entered Tiffany's apartment, carrying a cardboard tray of hot beverages in one hand. As the room was filled to the brim with Blaire's boxes, Mabel stubbed her toe on a large plastic container and lunged forward, nearly crashing to the floor. "What in the world? Did you bring everything you owned here?"

Sending Mabel a shrug, Blaire said, "What was I supposed to do? I couldn't take my stuff to my parent's house. I didn't think I could suffer through another lecture about my failure to meet their expectations. And I didn't bring everything here," emphasizing the word "everything."

Mabel's eyes widened. "Oh, really?" She scanned the room. "What did you leave behind? Lint?"

In an act of immaturity, Blaire stuck out her tongue at her friend. "Ha ha, very funny. For your information, I gave away my sofa and mattress. So, there." She crossed her arms in front of her chest for emphasis.

Chuckling, Mabel shook her head. "Only because those two things wouldn't fit in the SUV."

Blaire threw a nearby pillow from the couch at Mabel, who ducked despite still holding the drinks. Instead, the missile plowed into Tiffany's face, causing her to slosh her coffee all over the floor. "Oops. Sorry, Tiff."

Usually calm and steady, Tiffany's cheeks flushed a light pink color, now matching her shirt. "No problem. Listen, can we stop the bickering and shenanigans and get this show on the road? You know you leave tomorrow morning to live in another country for a month." She looked around the room before locking eyes again with Blaire. "As far as I can see, you aren't prepared at all. We have a lot of work to accomplish today."

Surprised by the stern tone in her usually gentle friend's voice, Blaire snapped into action. Fifteen minutes, one shower, and a dose of caffeine later, the trio headed out to conquer the day.

Tiffany turned to Blaire as the group started down the stairs to the apartment building's main floor. "I hate to say it, but if we're going to check off all the shopping on your list, we're going to have to take the subway. There's no way to hit all these stores on foot, and I can't afford a taxi. Come to think of it, neither can you."

A shiver traveled down Blaire's spine. *The subway*. She wasn't trying to be a subway snob—it was a quick, effective form of transportation. She just couldn't stand being so close to other people she didn't know. *Inhaling an assortment of germs*. Plus, given a choice between holding a high-touch railing versus falling on her face when the train moved, Blaire suspected she'd choose a face plant. "Do we have to take the subway?" Her eyes widened, pleading for another option.

Mabel turned around, a few steps in front of Blaire, and sent her a piercing stare. "Yes, we have to if you want to get everything done so you can get on that plane tomorrow. You can do it." She whipped her head forward again and continued down the stairs as if she'd settled the matter.

Sighing, Blaire patted her black bag containing a fresh set of wipes, a replacement for the purse she'd had stolen. Thankfully, she'd been able to notify her bank and credit card company before any harm had been done. As it turned out, she hadn't needed keys to her apartment any longer, so other than the loss of her time, it had been an easy fix. "Okay. I'll take the subway, but I'd feel better if I'd brought gloves, too."

In front of her, Blaire could see Mabel shaking her head. To

Mabel's credit, her straightforward friend kept her mouth shut.

Blaire followed her down the stairs and into the street in silence. She took a gulp of fresh air before boarding the subway.

Tiffany, Blaire, and Mabel underwent a shopping marathon, hitting the local health food store, pharmacy, and favorite clothing shop. They stopped only for a brief recharge at Tom's Coffee House at lunchtime. Blaire had nearly survived her retail outing unscathed when she heard someone call her name. Lifting her head, her eyes fell upon the last person she wanted to see.

In front of her stood Dr. Darren Byrne. "Blaire, I thought it was you. How are you doing?"

How was she doing? Her life was turned upside down. She'd lost her job and her apartment. And now her ex-boyfriend had a front-row seat to the aftermath. Other than that, just great. How was she doing? "Uh, I'm great." Blaire forced a smile on her face, but she wanted to sink into the floor.

Darren sent her a pitying look and a nod toward her mountain of bags. "Retail therapy?"

Her cheeks burned. *Who did Darren think he was suggesting she needed any kind of therapy? And so, what if she did? There was no shame in going to therapy, and it was none of his business.* She should've taken the high road and nodded and moved on. Instead, Blaire blurted out, "I'm preparing for a volunteer medical mission to Guatemala. I leave Sunday." *Ha, so there. Take that, Darren.*

His eyes widened, and a look of respect spread across his face. "Wow. That's great, Blaire. It's so...unlike you."

"What do you mean unlike—"

He raised a hand, cutting her off. "No offense intended. I meant it's hard to imagine you in a rural setting anywhere, much less in another country."

Any lingering thoughts of aborting her trip disappeared with Darren's obvious doubt about her capability. "Well, imagine away, because I'm going. In fact, I still have a lot to do, so I should be going."

Darren dipped his head in a small nod. "Okay, well…good luck."

"Thanks, but I won't need it." Blaire spun on her heel and rejoined her friends standing a few feet away. With each step, a bit of her false confidence slipped away.

"What was that about?" Mabel tilted her head toward Darren as he made a quick retreat.

Blaire sighed, and her shoulders sagged. "Oh, nothing. He simply stated what I was thinking…that this trip might be a crazy plan, and I'm going to be out of my depth."

Frowning, Mabel placed her armful of bags down and reached out to touch Blaire's arm. "Hey, none of that talk. I won't allow it. You're a strong woman, and this trip will be good for you. You'll make a difference and maybe learn to relax a little. Okay?" She raised a brow.

With a nod, Blaire agreed, "Okay." She gestured to the sacks she was lugging. "We better get home and try to fit all this stuff in my luggage."

Tiffany sent her a warm smile. "You got it. Let's go."

Armed with her supplies, Blaire followed her friends to Tiffany's apartment to pack and have a farewell dinner together.

Tiffany tried to talk her into taking the stairs, reminding her of what an excellent cardio workout it would be. Still, Blaire convinced her that eight hours of shopping and toting twenty bags bought them a one-way ticket up the building's elevator. Once all three girls boarded, Blaire kicked the button with her foot.

Mabel sighed. "You're going to break an elevator doing that one day."

"Maybe, but at least I won't contract the plague." Blaire smiled sweetly at her serious friend.

Once inside the safety of Tiffany's apartment, Blaire dropped her bags, whisked out a spray bottle of sanitizer, and misted herself head to toe as if trying out a new perfume.

Tiffany hacked and coughed, doubling over. "Bla-Blaire. Ca-

can't you l-let that g-go for o-once," she sputtered.

Knowing her friend well, Mabel had sidestepped to avoid Blaire's spray. She smirked. "Nope. She can't."

Blaire gave both friends a frown. "I'm going to let your criticism slide today, but only because my flight leaves at eight in the morning, and I need your help packing."

Mabel moved further into the living room. "Do you have a list of what you need to bring? Did the clinic director give suggestions?"

Reaching into her bag, Blaire dug around until her hand found the small folded piece of paper that she'd printed out the day prior. "Here it is." She reviewed it for the millionth time.

TO: blairecunningham7@ny.met.city.net
FROM: felipemartinez12@clinic.med.net
SUBJECT: La Clinica physician position

Dr. Cunningham,
  I'm looking forward to your arrival on the 787 New Horizons Flight arriving in Guatemala City at 1:30 pm. I plan to pick you up myself and will be waiting for you at the arrival's hub. Please let me know if you have any last-minute questions.
Sincerely,
Felipe Martinez, La Clinica Clinic Director

TO: felipemartinez12@clinic.med.net
FROM: blairecunningham7@ny.met.city.net
SUBJECT: packing list suggestions

Mr. Martinez,
  Thank you for the update. I do have a few questions. How many pieces of luggage may I bring? I know it sounds like a lot, but I think I'll need at least four to five large suitcases as I intend to bring some cleaning supplies of my

own as well as a few materials for the clinic. I may also bring some pre-packaged food items. Also, could you give me an itemized list of things you think may be helpful to gather?

Sincerely,

Dr. Blaire Cunningham

TO: blairecunningham7@ny.met.city.net

FROM: felipemartinez12@clinic.med.net

SUBJECT: packing list suggestions

Dr. Cunningham,

Five pieces of luggage might be too many, but I'll leave that up to you. My vehicle will accommodate it, but I should warn you that the guest room at the clinic is on the smaller side, so I'm not sure five bags will fit. I don't think bringing food or cleaning supplies of your own will be necessary. The most important thing to get is sunscreen, bug-spray, durable clothing and scrubs, sturdy close-toed shoes, and a sun hat. You may want swimwear and some towels, as the local lake is nice, too.

Sincerely,

Felipe Martinez, La Clinica Medical Director

Raising her head to meet Mabel's gaze, Blaire frowned. "Well, this list the clinic director sent me wasn't thorough, so I made my own. She flipped the paper over.

1. *Hand sanitizer*
2. *Back-up soap*
3. *Towels*
4. *Clean-All Wipes*
5. *More Clean-All Wipes*
6. *More hand sanitizer*
7. *Shampoo*

   8. *Scrubs*
   9. *Tennis shoes*
10. *Heels*
11. *Dress pants and tops*
12. *Maxi skirts*
13. *Gloves*
14. *Antibiotics*
15. *Granola bars*
16. *Peanut butter*
17. *Sunscreen*
18. *Swimwear*
19. *Hat*
20. *Sunglasses*

Mabel reached toward Blaire, her open palm awaiting the list. "Can I take a look?"

Wanting to delay her best friend's review of her packing list, Blaire paused. She met Mabel's even stare.

Mabel raised her forehead and stretched her hand out further. "Give it."

Sighing, Blaire handed the paper over. She didn't understand why people gave her a hard time about her...tendencies. So, she liked organization, cleanliness, and perfection, who didn't? It wasn't a crime, was it? "Before you say anything, I want to point out that I'm going to be in Guatemala for a least a month, and I don't know what will be available there. I'm a responsible planner." Not agreeing with her defense, she stared down at the ground.

Mabel skimmed the sheet, muttering each item to herself one by one. When she got to the third listing of hand sanitizer, she raised her head. A smile tugged at the corner of her lips. "It's worse than I thought." She crumpled the paper and tossed it to the floor. Walking to Blaire, she extended a hand to Blaire, helping her friend rise. "Come on, we have lots to do before you leave. If we pack nonstop, maybe we can get you ready in time."

Shaking her head, Blaire tried to resist her friend's offer. "I can handle this myself."

While she was talking, the sound of a tea kettle whistled, and the aroma of freshly roasted coffee beans wafted through the air. Blaire peered toward the kitchen and found Tiffany bustling between the stovetop and the coffee maker. Inhaling the calming scent, Blaire caved. "Okay. Maybe you're right. If I'm going to do this, I'm going to need the help of my two best friends. But I'm keeping all the hand sanitizer in my bag. And the wipes. That's nonnegotiable."

Mabel reached forward to shake Blaire's hand, but Blaire had already spritzed it with a cleansing spray. Instead, Blaire made an air high-five gesture to her two friends, who reciprocated, although Mabel shook her head while doing so.

The three women bustled around Tiffany's kitchen and living room carrying items from their recent retail excursion, packing until past midnight.

The sun peeked through half-closed vinyl blinds on Tiffany's apartment's sole window, rousing the troops. Tiffany smiled and stretched her arms as Blaire lifted her head from the couch, where she'd fallen asleep while reviewing her mental packing list. It was like the Clean-All version of counting sheep. By the time she got to Clean-All spray, Clean-All foam, and Clean-All wipes, she'd dozed off and hadn't budged all night.

Rubbing her eyes and yawning, Blaire glanced at the other end of the couch and found Mabel sleeping, her face buried into a pillow. Blaire rose from the sofa and tip-toed to the corner of the living room housing her luggage.

Staring at the bulging bags before her, Blaire placed a hand to her forehead in consternation. She turned to Tiffany, who appeared next to her, holding two mugs filled to the brim with black coffee. Accepting one of the cups from her considerate friend, Blaire returned her thoughts to her upcoming journey, wondering what lay ahead. She took a long sip of the hot drink, letting it warm her worried soul and sighed. "I don't know," she spoke, still looking at the bags, not yet meeting the gaze of her friend.

Tiffany took a draw off her mug, too, before responding, "What don't you know?"

Blaire met Tiffany's gaze while holding her cup with a tight grip as if it might provide her with courage or clarity. "I don't know what I'm doing. I don't know if I'll make it. I don't know if I can handle being a physician at this rural clinic. Maybe everyone else is right about me; my parents, Dr. Sedgewick, even Darren. Maybe I'm too germaphobic, too perfectionistic, too rigid to be a doctor…especially one who deals with infectious disease."

A hand settled on Blaire's right shoulder, startling her. Blaire turned, and a pool of empathy filled Mabel's eyes, replacing her usual direct stare.

A slow smile of encouragement spread across Mabel's face. "Hey, you've got this. Don't worry about what everyone else thinks. Your parents are…your parents."

Blaire snorted. "You've got that right. High expectations and a low tolerance for failure."

Mabel pointed to herself and Tiffany with her other hand. "We believe in you. We know you can do it. It might not be easy… that's true. But anything worth doing is usually hard."

Tiffany placed a hand on Blaire's other shoulder and gave it a squeeze. "She's right." Her mouth fell into a taut line, and she frowned before uttering, "The state rests."

Blaire snickered and glanced at Mabel to see if she would crack, too.

Although her eyes clouded, a smile started to form. Mabel chuckled, and within seconds all three friends had erupted into a full-on giggle fit.

Once the laugher subsided, Blaire wiped away the happy tears from the corner of her eye. "Oh, thanks for that, girls. I needed it. Now, back to the matter at hand. Are thirty packs of Clean-All Wipes too many?"

Chapter 13

"Don't Get Your Knickers in a Twist"

Blaire spent Saturday packing with her two best friends and capped the night off with a delicious dinner from Tony's Pizzeria around the corner of Tiffany's apartment. Thankfully, it also got one of the highest health code ratings, which pleased Blaire.

She crashed early Saturday evening and made it to the airport Sunday morning three hours earlier than her flight's departure time. Blaire liked to plan ahead and left nothing to chance. The flight presented its own challenges; the tray tables and armrests needed to be cleaned, which garnered her a few odd looks. Although she tried to avoid the airplane bathroom, a seven-hour flight made it impossible. Fortunately, she brought plenty of wipes and gave everything a thorough scrub. Unfortunately, this led to her spending an unusual amount of time in the plane's closet-size bathroom, which garnered her even more strange looks upon exiting.

Listening to soothing music enabled her to complete the trip with only one near-panic attack. Once safely on the ground, she exited the plane and found baggage claim, along with all five pieces of her luggage. It looked like she intended to stay much longer than a month—maybe a year. She found a rickety metal cart and loaded her bags onto it. It created a mound so high, she couldn't see over the top while pushing it.

Once she'd made it to the arrivals waiting area outside the yellow and tan airport, she saw a concrete bench. Blaire rustled through her purse and extracted a wipe and gave the surface a swipe before flopping down. Once seated, Blaire couldn't peer over her stacked bags, but glancing at her phone, she speculated she had another ten or fifteen minutes before her ride came. She rested her chin on her fist and leaned forward. A gentle breeze blew, bringing a welcome wave of relief along with the warm scent of vanilla.

She closed her eyes and allowed her shoulders to relax. She said a prayer of thanks to God for landing, even though the small plane had tumbled around like a kernel in a popcorn machine.

A raucous noise disrupted her blissful moment. She raised her head and saw a billow of dust around either side of her luggage tower. *Was that a chicken she heard? No, not possible.* She shook her head. Blaire rose and smoothed out the front of her pressed khaki capris. She wanted to make a good impression, so she wore her favorite blouse--a delicate white button-up short sleeve top over a tank top underneath. She'd paired the outfit with black kitten heels to boost her confidence and make herself look taller.

Blaire pushed a rogue strand of hair out of her eyes and tucked it behind her ear. As the wind picked up, she wished she'd put her hair in a ponytail. Beads of perspiration coalesced around the back of her neck from the humid, eighty-some degree temperature. She retrieved a tissue from her bag and patted it across her forehead before tossing it in her purse.

She stepped forward and teetered on her heels, pushing all of her weight into the luggage cart. As the wonky column nearly toppled over, she shoved the top suitcase into place and resumed moving her monolith forward.

Blaire stopped at the curb of the gate and peeked around the steeple of luggage. Her jaw fell open. In front of her stood a wooden ten-foot-long truck with at least four stacked boxes holding...*chickens?* The truck's back was open-air and constructed of several horizontal stacked planks of wood with a black metal railing overhead, connecting the truck's front to the back. Plastered on the side of the truck were the words, "Jose's Farm." *Who was Jose?*

A tall, broad-shouldered man threw open the driver side door of the beat-up forest green truck and ambled out of it. He wore a straw hat covering his face, dirty jeans, and a tight black t-shirt that stretched across a firm, well-muscled chest. Shutting the truck door with a tanned arm, he lifted his head. The man tilted his hat and revealed familiar rich, deep chocolate brown eyes.

They were the same eyes as the man she'd rescued on the street in New York City! *How could this be? How could the man in the suit she'd saved from a bus be the same person standing before her?* Blaire tried to ignore the pounding in her chest as her pulse quickened at the sight of the handsome man.

The chicken truck driver took in the brunette wearing heels and pressed, pristine clothes along with the tower of luggage. Recognition flashed across his face as he removed his hat and ran a hand through his ebony curls. He gave her a small nod. "Wow. Small world." Tilting his head toward her stuff, he asked, "Is this all yours?"

Blaire glanced at her suitcases, taking stock. *It did look like a lot, but she was staying for a month. A month! And who was this person to question her packing?* "Yes, why?"

Instead of answering, the man shoved a hand in his front jean pocket and dug out a piece of paper. "You're Dr. Cunningham? Dr. Blaire Cunningham?"

No. No way. This couldn't be her ride. She was not riding in the back of that truck. With extreme caution in her voice, Blaire replied, "Ye-yes. Who are you?"

"I'm Felipe. Felipe Martinez. We spoke via email. I'm the clinic director." He stepped forward and stretched out a hand dirtied with grease, ready to shake Blaire's.

She stared at his hand and froze. Extending a trembling hand, she grasped only the tips of his fingers and gave them a quick tug before snapping her hand back like a turtle heading into its shell. "Nice to meet you...officially. And to see you again. I hope you're abiding by crosswalk laws nowadays." She slipped her hand into her purse and rooted around for a wipe. She rubbed her contaminated fingers against it with all the discretion she could muster while maintaining a forced smile on her face.

He chuckled. "Yeah, that was a crazy day. Thanks again."

Although her handshake with Felipe had been brief, her fingertips tingled from his touch. Warmth flooded her neck and cheeks, and her palms began to sweat. Despite her sympathetic system's unexpected betrayal, she resolved to focus on the task at hand--completing her work at the clinic and heading home as soon as possible to reclaim her fellowship spot. Besides, irritation crept in as she considered her current mode of transportation. She could hear her mother's voice in her head, *This is how you're going to spend your time? Gallivanting across the globe in a chicken truck? You are a Cunningham. When are you going to act like one?"*

Clearing her throat, Blaire tried to regain her composure. *Did Felipe expect her to board this...chariot?* She squinted and raised a hand to her forehead, shading her eyes from the scorching afternoon sun. *And was there a dog in the passenger seat?* She scrunched her eyes tighter, looking for confirmation. *Yep, there was a canine riding shotgun. Great. So, did he expect her to ride in the back?*

Felipe surveyed the luggage tower next to Blaire and gestured with his thumb toward it, still holding his hat in the other hand. "So, these bags--"

Defensive, Blaire stammered, "Ye-yes. I know it looks like a lot—"

Shaking his head, Felipe cut in, "Looks like a lot? It is a lot." He shifted his glance between the suitcases and the bed of the truck as if trying to determine if everything would fit. "You're only committed to the clinic for a month, right?" He sent her a quizzical look.

Becoming more indignant, Blaire crossed her arms. "That's right. But what you don't understand is not all the items in these bags are for me."

The handsome man smirked. "Oh, yeah? Who are they for, then?"

Blaire's face burned. *How dare he make fun of her? Sure, she had not "packed light."* Her friends had rallied and helped her get ready. They'd pressed scrubs, packed bright white tennis shoes, antibiotics, sanitizer, a box of soap, iodine tablets, ten bottles of sunscreen, vitamins, and astronaut food. Yep, dehydrated space food. Perhaps, it wasn't practical, but she had wanted to prepare for any circumstance. "I brought things for the clinic, too," she said, narrowing her eyes.

Her newfound acquaintance and growing adversary's smirk spread into a broad grin. He snorted and tried to cover it by placing a hand in front of his mouth as if to rub his jaw. "Well, then the clinic thanks you. I hate to cut our conversation short, but we need to get a move on it. Afternoon traffic on the main road can be…hectic. We want to avoid it if possible." He glanced over his shoulder at the truck cab and his passenger in the front seat before meeting Blaire's gaze again. "I hate to ask you to do this…but Pedro is old and doesn't do well riding in the back. I was hoping you wouldn't mind…sitting back there."

Her mouth fell open. "You want me to ride in the open air down the highway? Is that safe? Or legal?"

Felipe sent her a half-grin. "Well, it's not ideal, I'll give you that, but I'll mainly drive on back roads. Not much traffic on those.

Besides, it's so hot today, the breeze will feel better than riding up front. I borrowed the truck from my buddy. The clinic's van is out of commission right now." He nodded to the front of the truck. "The AC is broken, and it's a hot box up there. Plus, the truck bed has a bench you can sit on, and if we go too fast for your liking, you can grab the bar overhead."

Blaire closed her eyes and whispered a silent prayer. Although convinced this car ride might lead to her demise, she didn't see any other choice besides hopping the next plane out of here. Returning home, she'd face a disappointed Mabel and a smug Stella Cunningham, wearing an "I-told-you-so" grin on her face. No, like it or not, Blaire had a date with a chicken truck. She hoped it would be her last. Opening her eyes, she said a flat, "Great." *Just great.*

Chapter 14

"Never Judge a Book by Its Cover"

Slamming the door shut, Felipe settled into the driver seat of the cab. He placed his hat next to him, rousing his canine friend.

Pedro lifted his brown and white spotted head and tilted it as if to say, "What do you think of her?"

Reaching over, Felipe scratched behind the ear of his longtime friend and leaned closer. "I don't know, buddy. I don't think she's going to last a month. I'll be surprised if she makes it a week. Did you see her shoes? Who goes on a rural medical trip in heels?"

The dog raised his brow a bit higher in response.

"I know I should give her a chance, but she seems like a...city-slicker. And even a bit snobby. I wouldn't call that a handshake she gave me if you paid me." He peered over his shoulder at the beautiful young woman sitting in the back of his borrowed truck. "Maybe she'll be a pleasant surprise. And like my grandmother used to say, "Beggars can't be choosers." She's buying me and the clinic time, and she does have good credentials on her resumé.

The woman patted another cloth to her face and neck before pushing loose tendrils into the ponytail she'd fixed during his conversation with a dog. He much preferred the relaxed look those strands gave her. They softened her face and glowed in the late afternoon sunlight.

Dr. Blaire Cunningham had caught him off guard. He didn't know why, but based on the emails she'd sent him, he'd expected to pick up someone…older and much less…attractive. What Felipe said to Pedro held true; he doubted her ability to survive here based on their brief interaction and the mountain of luggage. He wanted to focus on enduring the month, taking whatever help she could offer. He'd return her to the airport at the month's end and be done with her. But something nagged at him. Her deep blue eyes drew him in, and his heartbeat quickened at her brief touch. Even now, he found her frustration somewhat endearing.

Pedro yawned, apparently bored with the conversation, and returned to his original position with his head resting atop his two muddy paws.

"Sorry I'm boring you, but you're right. We need to go." With that final thought, Felipe planted his foot on the clutch and brake and turned the key. He grabbed the stick and shoved it into gear and pulled forward with caution. Tossing a glance behind him once more, Felipe made sure he hadn't already lost his puzzling passenger and clinic savior. Seeing that she had a firm grip on one of the rails, he drove off, kicking a fresh wave of dust into the air.

Chapter 15

"Flying by the Seat of Her Pants"

Still clutching her chest, Blaire attempted to regain enough breath to spew the angry words she'd been formulating during her death-defying ride to the clinic. She sighed. The truck had stopped. She unclenched her eyes and found herself staring at the front of a simple, grey cinder block building. It stood two stories high, with two small windows on each level. Dirty with years of neglect, a lone wooden door shone as the sole beacon of beauty. Although a thin layer of grime covered the door, intricate carvings around the edges made it unique. She imagined it could tell some stories.

Attached to the main building was a smaller one-story version on the left side and a similar one on the right. The one to the right bore a sign reading, "Internet Café" in red letters.

The dust surrounding the truck announced their arrival. As it settled, Blaire relaxed her white-knuckle grip on the plank behind her. At one point in the trip, she'd convinced herself the end was near. She suspected they'd traveled upwards of fifty miles an hour, which under normal circumstances (in a car with working seat restraints and a roof and windows) wouldn't have been a problem. However, barreling down a bumpy dirt road with the wind in her face had not produced the calming effect Felipe promised. Quite the opposite, in fact. Thinking about him and his dog sitting safely in the front seat of the cab made her jaw tighten.

A voice broke through her reverie, "Ready to hop down?" Felipe extended a hand to her, offering his assistance.

Blaire lifted her head and locked eyes with Felipe. She hoped he felt the heat emanating from her stare. "I can get down by myself, thank you very much." She sniffed and patted her hair. It felt like a billowing cloud atop her head, thanks to the wind tunnel she'd ridden through.

A teasing glint danced in Felipe's eyes, and he stepped aside. "Suit yourself. You've got a little something right there," he said, pointing to her cheek.

She raised a brow and muttered, "Huh?" before stepping down from the end of the truck with caution. She shuffled to the front of the vehicle and peeked into a rusted side mirror. Blaire gasped. "I look awful." The reflection before her revealed a woman unhinged. She had a black mark of dirt or some other heinous substance smeared across her right cheek, and her hair frizzed above her head, resembling a bird's nest. She attempted to smash it into submission, but, after a few unsuccessful attempts, relented.

Felipe's face appeared in the mirror's hazy reflection next to hers. He barely concealed a grin. "Ready to see the clinic and your room?"

Blaire gave one final glance at herself and shrugged. "Sure, why not. Let me grab my bags." She reached for the most oversized suitcase, but a firm, warm hand on her forearm stopped her. A shiver traveled down her spine, and she caught her breath.

Smiling with sincerity this time, Felipe stopped her. "I'll get that one." He gathered four of her largest bags, leaving the small one and her carry-on for her to manage. "I should warn you there are stairs to your room."

Even though he'd lightened her load, Blaire still struggled. She placed her purse across her body, slung her carry-on on one shoulder, and heaved the other two bags into each hand. Buried under the weight of her poor decision making, Blaire teetered into the clinic. As she stepped through the massive wooden door, a waft of stale air intermixed with dark coffee overcame her. She resisted the urge to cough as dust particles filled her lungs, not able to afford a sneeze under the burden of her bags. "Can we sit these down in my room first," she sputtered.

Felipe turned around to see her straining and nodded. "Sure. It's this way." He led her down a narrow concrete hallway painted a medium brown color. The overall effect was dungeon-like.

Approaching a set of shallow stairs, Blaire paused. She gingerly placed one foot on a stair as if she were testing the water in a hot bath. When her entire body didn't crash through the ancient wood, she continued up the stairwell behind Felipe.

At the top step, he scooted to the side, making room for Blaire.

It appeared there were only two rooms on the upper level; one to the right side of the hallway and one opposite it on the left.

Felipe nodded to the room on the right. "That's my room. I get room and board and an additional stipend from the city in exchange for the work I do running the clinic." Then, he tilted his head to the room on the left side of the hallway. "And that's where you'll stay. It's the extra room reserved for volunteer staff and sometimes used as storage space, too." He met her gaze and must have seen concern in them. "Don't worry, I cleaned it out before you came, so it's not a storage shed."

Blaire sighed. She trudged behind him and plopped her bags on the ground, thankful to be rid of her load. Rolling her wrists and shaking out her sore hands, Blaire scanned her abode. She stifled a gasp. *How could she live here for a month?*

In front of her, displayed in all its cement glory, was her new home.

Felipe led the way into the room, rubbing the back of his neck. "I know it's probably not what you're used to in New York."

She rubbed her eyes, hoping things would look better when she opened them. Nope. The dark grey concrete floor, similar to the clinic below, held an inch-thick layer of dust as if no one dared disturb the dirt. She squinted her eyes. *Was that a deceased bug on the floor near the bed? Yep. A dead bug.* Blaire started to hyperventilate. "Is…that…a…bug?"

Felipe stifled a laugh before placing a hand on her back, patting her. Sarcasm dripped from his voice, "Take a deep breath. Calm down. It's dead. Can't hurt you now. I hate to tell you, but there are lots of bugs here. Especially spiders."

Blaire twisted her face in disgust, trying to take slow, even breaths. She shook her head and attempted to shift to a more positive mindset. *It will be okay.* A rumpled red and purple handwoven quilt lay atop the twin-size bed pushed against a wall. The middle of the far wall held one small window. A layer of filth covered it, so a ray of sunshine would have to fight like a ninja to burst forth any light.

On the wall opposite the bed, a thin door held what Blaire assumed to be a small closet. Next to the bed sat a slim wooden nightstand with an old-fashioned oil lamp atop its scratched surface. After scanning the room, Blaire noted the cobwebs hanging in the corners of the ceiling. Oh, and their creators were still there, too. Her knees weakened, the room spun, and she thought she might faint.

The rugged, gorgeous man stood upright and gave her a grim smile. "Listen, it's not too late to return to the airport and catch a plane home." He raised his brows and gestured around him. "This life, this place…I love it, and it's my home, but it may not be for everyone. No hard feelings if you've changed your mind."

Blaire paused and closed her eyes, thinking for a minute. She couldn't give up now. She was determined to stick to her commitment, help some people, finish the month out, and win her fellowship spot back. No matter what. Raising up, Blaire squared her shoulders. She shook her head with vigor, saying, "No. No way I'm leaving. I made a promise to you and this clinic, and I'm a woman of my word." After all, it's a month. She could do anything for a month.

He tilted his head and stared at her for a few seconds before breaking into a wide grin. "Okay, then. Why don't you get unpacked, and when you're done, come downstairs? I'll give you a complete tour of the rest of the clinic."

Her shoulders relaxed, and she nodded. She couldn't wait to change out of her dusty, sweat-ridden clothes into something fresh. However, she suspected with the humidity, it wouldn't matter much. "Thanks, that'd be great. I'll be down soon."

Felipe turned to leave his new colleague to her task, and the room fell silent.

Surveying the room once more, Blaire made a mental list of everything she needed to do to whip the place into shape. The first order of business was apparent; clean everything. She needed a mop and broom to do a thorough job, but she didn't see those items. She unzipped the heaviest suitcase. Pulling out gloves, a face mask, and the linchpin, bleach wipes, she clapped her hands in glee.

While scrubbing the floor and nightstand, Blaire pondered how best to remove the arthropodic nemeses from the corners of the room. Two sets of shoes thrown with fair aim managed to knock the creatures out of their hiding places and lead to their demise.

Two hours and three Clean-All Wipe packs later, she pulled her gloves off and tossed them in a small trash bin in her room, along with her mask. She planted her hands on her hips and grinned. Although not quite to the Blaire Cunningham standard of "clean," she still considered the room a vast improvement. She made a note to ask Felipe about a broom and mop. *Oh, and bleach. Lots and lots of bleach.* With that final thought, she gave her hands a spritz of sanitizer and headed downstairs to see what else Felipe and La Clinica had in store for her.

Chapter 16

"We're Not Laughing with You"

Felipe plodded down the dark staircase to the main floor of the clinic below. How would she last a month? She'd barely survived the road from the city to the small-town housing the community clinic. When he witnessed her panic attack upstairs, he'd considered piling her luggage into the borrowed truck and hightailing her to the mothership of New York City. But he needed her, like it or not. And right now, he did not like it. He sighed and headed to his small office to be alone and think.

He bumped into Juanita, near the tiny kitchenette housed in the clinic's rear on the way to the office. He smiled at his longtime friend and colleague. "Hey Juanita, how's it going?"

She stood stooped over the metal stovetop, frying an egg in a black cast iron pan. With her silvering hair piled on her head and an apron tied around her plump middle, she reminded him of his grandmother.

Peeking to the side, she sent Felipe a smile, never stopping her hands from their busied task. "I'm good. I was busy all morning, taking phone calls and setting up the schedule for the week. So, now I'm taking a break." Even though Juanita lived within walking distance of the clinic, she was not one to miss a meal. So, it made sense she gave a late lunch priority over finishing early and heading home. With her hands still at work on the pan in front of her, she looked up, meeting Felipe's gaze. "So, how did it go? What's the big city doctor like?"

Chuckling, Felipe shook his head. "About like you might expect. She brought a thousand bags, each weighing a ton, wore high heels, and nearly fainted at the sight of her room. Thought I was going to have to give her medical attention because of a bug on the floor." He snorted.

Juanita flipped off the knob to the stove and slid her sunny side up egg onto a worn teal-colored plate. The aroma of peppers and onions filled the air. She grabbed a knife from a nearby basket and carried the dish to the kitchen table. The table could accommodate four people but only had three chairs. She plopped her plate on the table and pulled out a seat, nodding for Felipe to join her. "Sit down."

Given the authority in her voice, he obeyed. "Yes, ma'am." He sent her a mischievous grin.

"I've known you for a long time…and I understand how important this clinic is to you and why you do it. It's important to me, too. A lot is riding on the next month and if this young lady works out or not. But," she paused, taking a bite and chewing before continuing, "you've got to give her a chance."

"I am—"

Pointing her fork at Felipe, Juanita cut him off, "You are not. I'm sure she's overwhelmed right now. This way of life," she gestured in the air with her fork, "is special and beautiful, but I'm sure it's much different than her home." She pierced another piece of egg, finishing off her meal. "And who knows, maybe she'll fall in love and stay."

Felipe felt his throat tighten. "Fall in love?" he croaked.

Now it was Juanita's turn to smirk. "With the town and its people, of course."

His shoulders sagged, and he hoped his face wasn't as emblazoned as it felt. "Of course," he agreed.

Stacking her fork on the plate, Juanita rose and carried her items to the sink, gave them a quick wash with soap and water before placing them in the drying rack. She wiped her hands on the front of her apron before untying it and hanging it on a hook on the wall. Turning to face Felipe, she grinned. "Well, I'm heading home, but be ready to work hard tomorrow. I received several calls and walk-ins today, and the list is packed. I hope your young physician can hit the ground fast."

A welcome cool breeze blew through the open window next to the stove. It brought with it a reprieve from the unabating humidity of the Guatemalan summer and the scent of rain attached to one of the frequent midday storms. He closed his eyes and sighed. When he opened them again, Juanita had gone. He whispered, "I hope she can, too."

Chapter 17

"We're Laughing at You"

Blaire awoke early, after suffering through a night with her quilt pulled up to her eyeballs and little sleep for fear of a bug, spider, or other creature crawling across her face. She shuddered at the thought, slipping her feet into flip-flops on the cement ground below. She recalled college days of wearing shower shoes to avoid contracting some horrifying disease.

Rubbing her eyes, she looked around the room. Yep. She was still here. It wasn't a dream. She picked up her phone from the nightstand and looked to see if she had service. No bars. She'd sent a quick text message to her parents yesterday when she'd landed to let them know she was alive.

Her mother's response was typical and concise, "Great. Thanks." *So nurturing.*

Blaire also messaged Mabel and Tiffany, stating she'd arrived in one piece and only removed her skin's first layer from scouring it with disinfectant during her journey. Well, that was an exaggeration, but really, not by much. She glanced at her arms and hands, a light pink from her efforts at decontamination. She shrugged.

Tiffany had replied with a heartfelt, "Praying for your safety and success. Love you!"

Mabel took her direct approach, "Good to hear from you. Don't panic. You'll be fine. And don't clean everything in sight."

Blaire hoped to call or message them later. Perhaps she could slip over to the internet café or see if the clinic had wifi. Rising, she shuffled out of her room and down the hallway to the bathroom. Since she shared it with Felipe, she knocked first. Leaning her head against the door to listen for an answer, she waited. Hearing none, she pushed the door open and slipped in with her caddy in tow.

Felipe took her on a clinic tour the day prior. He'd showed her the main room with its grey concrete floor, cinder block walls, unfinished ceiling, and overhead fluorescent lights. A hallway connected the clinic to the kitchen, if you could call it that based on its size. Two dust-covered windows shielded any natural light from entering the space. A closet-sized room Felipe claimed as his office and the upstairs bathroom completed the tour. So, it wasn't her first time seeing the bathroom. That didn't lessen the shock.

The bathroom itself looked clean, other than a few cobwebs in the corners. The most daunting part of the room stood in the center-- an old clawfoot tub with a sagging dingy shower curtain surrounding it. Above the middle of the tub resided a metal arm holding the showerhead and a curious metal coil. When Blaire had asked Felipe what purpose it served, he'd laughed.

"Oh, that. Don't touch that. Ever."

That's all he said about it and carried on with the tour. She placed her caddy on the floor next to the makeshift shower and locked the door behind her. Stepping into the shower, she steadied herself by holding the edge of the tub. Once inside, she tossed her robe over the back end, hoping it would stay dry, and turned the rusted knob at the front of the tub to the right. The metal pipe running up the middle of the cauldron toward the ceiling groaned, and at first, she wondered if it might burst.

After a few seconds, the pipe came to life, and ice-cold water sprung forth, spraying her in the face. The smell of sulfur and the shock of the icy blast caused her to gasp. "Agh!" She struggled to find the knob to make the water hot or turn it off. Twisting the knob on the left created a new pinging sound, and she hoped the glacial shower would be righted.

The water turned lukewarm, an improvement, but did not heat beyond that. Oddly, it alternated between warm and ice-cold, never deciding on a permanent temperature. Blaire looked up to find the pinging's loudest source and noted a red tinge to the coil atop the showerhead. *How strange.*

A voice deep within whispered to her not to touch it, and she paused with her hand hanging in the air. Ignoring the self-warning, she extended her fingers, attempting to tweak the red coil above. *Zap.* "Ouch!" It sent out a jolt, and her fingers tingled. *What in the world is that?*

Done with her attempt at a peaceful moment, she yanked on the two handles until the flow of water ceased. *There. Take that.* She frowned at the offending agent overhead. "That's the last time you'll get me."

Hopping out of the porcelain basin of electroshock therapy, Blaire dried off and threw her robe on before trudging down the hall to her room. She shimmied into a black maxi dress and slid her feet into matching leather wedges with a cork heel.

After a few strokes of her hairbrush, Blaire pulled her damp hair into a low ponytail. She glanced around the room for a mirror. Not finding one, she slipped a small compact out of her purse. A quick glimpse confirmed her suspicion; frizzy hair and beads of sweat abounded. *Oh, well.* Her eyes fell upon the travel-size hand sanitizer bottle in her bag, and she smiled. She poured a dab of it in her hands and rubbed them together, inhaling the scent of absolute clean. *Ah.*

Better.

Blaire made her bed and zipped up her suitcases so no adventurous creatures would make themselves at home in her things, and then headed downstairs for breakfast.

Yesterday, Felipe sprung on her the news that the clinic would open today with patients to see if she felt up to it. A flurry of butterflies twisted around in her stomach, and while she didn't know if she'd last the month, she felt excited to have a purpose again. Although the germs involved with medicine gave her a fright most days, she still loved the science of it all.

At the bottom of the stairs, she bumped into Felipe, and a surge of warmth spread to her cheeks. She started to smile, but then recalled her near-electrocution earlier. Furrowing her brow, she wagged a finger at him. "Hey, do you know your shower almost killed me?"

He raised a quizzical brow and replied, "Good morning to you, too. Now, what are you talking about?"

"I said, your shower almost ended my life today. I nearly had a heart attack, or an arrhythmia, or something. There I stood in an artic shower, minding my own business, and the crazy coil thing on top wouldn't heat the water and made a funny sound...so I twisted it."

He chuckled and raised a hand. "Wait, wait. Don't tell me you touched the electrical heating coil." He paused and waited for her to refute his accusation. When she remained mute, he continued on in his lecture. "That's why it's called an electrical heating coil. Because it's electricity. As in, electricity and water don't mix."

She put her hands on her hips and shifted her weight. "I'm a doctor. I know about science. Of course, I wouldn't have touched it if I knew it had electricity flowing through it. Besides, why would anyone put an electrical coil next to water? Isn't that dangerous?"

Laughing louder now, Felipe tried to catch his breath and sputtered a few words, "No...that's... how...it's...designed." He drew in a long breath and exhaled it slowly, shaking his head. "You're funny. I told you not to touch that thing yesterday during our tour. Don't you remember?"

Angry over his amusement at her near-death experience, she sent him a glare. "No, I didn't remember, or I wouldn't have touched it, would I?" She spun on her heel and stomped down the hallway to the kitchen.

Felipe continued laughing as he followed behind her and muttered something about her being a "city-slicker."

Who does he think he is? It was an honest mistake. Blaire reached for a mug and poured piping hot black coffee from a glass carafe into her cup. She untied a bag of bread and tossed a piece of it onto a plate. Pulling the handle attached to the worn, white refrigerator caused the door to open and let out a moan. She scanned the shelves looking for jelly or butter, but, finding none, shut the door.

Blaire surveyed the counter for sugar and said a thankful prayer when her eyes landed on a dark blue sugar bowl. A lid sat atop it, and a small ceramic spoon lay inside a notched edge. She lifted the lid and screamed. Tiny black ants marched across the top of the sugar mound as if they'd claimed it as their colony. "What is this?" she exclaimed, pointing to the offending insects.

He scrutinized the bowl in question and met her gaze. "What? It's a sugar bowl." He busied himself with getting his own cup of coffee and retrieving a hard-boiled egg from the fridge.

"It's an infested sugar bowl. It's contaminated. We can't eat this. Who knows what countless germs they're carrying?" She paused, thinking. "E. coli, for one. Staph, Strep...I think even Shigella. Do you know what Shigella can do to you? Do you?" Blaire slammed the lid down on the sugar bowl, waiting for Felipe's response.

Felipe sat his plate and mug on the table and took a seat. He dug into his egg and spoke between bites, "No. Contrary to your belief, it is not my goal to make everyone in the clinic, particularly you, die or take ill. I am a medic, you know. I know about the Hippocratic oath. But I'm not panicking about a few ants."

She crossed her arms. "Fine. I'll drink my coffee black." She pointed to her cup before picking it up. "This is made from purified, clean drinking water, I presume?"

With a flourish of his hand, Felipe dipped his head. "Of course, madam. Only the best for you."

Blaire decided to ignore his sarcastic tone and hope for the best, taking a cautious sip off her dark brew. *Mmm.* Well, at least the coffee didn't disappoint. In fact, it was delicious. She carried her mug and plate to the table and sat across from Felipe, eyeing him. She couldn't dispute his good looks. His dark hair, tanned skin, and half-smile almost made her forget her anger at him over the shower debacle. Almost.

Taking a bite of her dry toast, Blaire relaxed. "So, what's the plan for today? Do you have scheduled patients, or do people line up first-come, first-serve?"

With his plate already empty, Felipe plucked a napkin from the holder in the center of the table. He wiped his mouth before answering, "Well, we do a little of both. Juanita scheduled about fifteen to twenty patients for us to see today, but we often have walk-ins, too. Usually, another five to ten patients show up unannounced or with an emergency. There's a hospital in Guatemala City, but that's a few hours' drive by farming truck or horseback, which most people use here. Plus, the hospital can get expensive, and most of our patients won't seek care due to cost or inability to travel."

She nodded her head and took her last bite of toast and swig of coffee. "Okay. It sounds like we've got a full day ahead, so why don't you explain to me the flow of the clinic, and we can get started." Blaire tossed her napkin in the trash bin in the corner and ran water over her plate and dirty mug, stacking them in the rack. Turning around, she brushed a few crumbs off her shirt and righted herself.

Felipe rose from the table and sent her a grin. "Let's go." He exited the kitchen, already on his way to the central hub of the clinic.

Blaire remained behind, rooted in place with her cheeks still warm from his smile. *Stop that. There's no time for nonsense.* Besides, in a month, she'd be back to her former life of endless cleaning products, structure, and order. She stepped forward and entered the clinic she'd walked through only a day prior. In contrast, where the simple, concrete room once stood empty, it boasted a flurry of activity today.

To the right of her sat Juanita, stationed behind an eight-foot white folding table, checking in patients one at a time. The line formed across her table and trailed out the door, despite the early hour of eight a.m. It looked like the patients varied in age from as young as three or four up to seventy or more.

Juanita scribbled information on a stack of index cards in front of her, smiling and greeting each patient as if they were an old friend. Based on the size of the town, this was probably true.

On the opposite end of the clinic stood two exam rooms. Felipe stood waiting for her next to one of the rooms. He caught her eye and waved for her to join him.

She drew in a deep breath and marched onward, trying to portray a face bearing more confidence than she currently felt. "So, how do you want to do this?"

Holding a plastic clipboard and pen, Felipe scribbled something on a white lined index card. He lifted his head. "Usually, Juanita does the initial intake of the patient's history. She documents any changes in medications, allergies, that sort of thing."

Blaire nodded, marveling at the simplicity of the notecard system. "Wait, that's how you chart? On a notecard?"

He shrugged. "Hey, it works. So, like I said, she gets the patient chart started. Once they're checked in, she has them wait in the blue chairs lining the wall. Then, I call the patients to come back one at a time into an exam room." He pointed to the empty rooms behind him with his pen. "I take their vitals and notify you when they're ready to be seen."

She noted a stethoscope around Felipe's neck and a few instruments clipped within his pockets. "Sounds efficient." Blaire peered around the room and counted five people seated and waiting against the wall in chairs. "I guess we should go ahead and get started. It's packed." She pointed to the wall of chairs filled with patients.

He gave her a nod and led her to one of the open exam rooms.

She surveyed the cinderblock room, which, although clean, continued with the same brown and grey tones of the rest of the building. *A little gloomy, but at least no spiderwebs.* In the center of the room sat an old navy-blue exam table covered with a white paper strip. Blaire sat her purse on a makeshift wooden desk in the corner and dug through it, retrieving her wipes. She gave the desk a swipe and readied herself to tackle the exam table, but Felipe stopped her.

"Have a little faith in us. You can put that stuff away. We cleaned the table. It's not dirty." He chuckled. "And there's even hand sanitizer attached to the wall." He pointed to a cream container with a push pump on the wall.

Embarrassed that he'd pointed out one of her quirks, she attempted nonchalance. "Oh, I know." She tossed the packet of wipes into her purse and sat in the metal chair beside the desk. It rocked and groaned as she eased into it. She sent him a smile that didn't feel genuine, as she worried about the chair's reliability to hold her weight.

Crossing her hands in her lap, Blaire said, "Okay, I'm ready. Send in the first patient."

Felipe disappeared for a few minutes and returned with a dark, long-haired little girl behind him. She looked thinner than she should.

Blaire took the index card from Felipe and skimmed the information.

Name: Angel Marino
DOB: 3/31/2013
Medical History: malnutrition, failure to thrive, history of parasitosis
Allergies: None
Social History: lives with her nine siblings, parents

deceased, oldest sibling is her guardian
Chief Complaint: needs vitamins

Blaire sat the index card on the desk and turned to face her first patient.

The little girl stared at her, no light in her eyes.

Pulling a pair of gloves from a pack on the wall, Blaire donned them and stepped closer to the girl. "My name is Dr. Cunningham, but you can call me Dr. Blaire. It's nice to meet you." She extended a gloved hand to the girl.

The child looked at the new physician standing before her and remained motionless.

Putting her hand back down at her side, Blaire cleared her throat. "Ahem, well, okay, why don't we get started? It says on your card that you're here for vitamins. Is that correct?"

Felipe stepped forward, cutting her off. "If I may…she doesn't speak English."

Blaire's cheeks burned. "Right, of course. I'm sorry. Um, my Spanish is a little rusty…do you think you could stay and help translate?"

Smiling, Felipe nodded. "Sure." He turned to the girl and repeated Blaire's questions. Once he garnered her quiet response, he reiterated it to Blaire. "She says she needs vitamins because her family does not have a lot of food, and she wants to stay healthy. They eat mostly tortillas, but some days they have nothing."

Blaire peered at the girl, and her heart melted. Tears threatened to spill over, but she tamped them back down. "That's horrible. How can they not have food? Isn't there a food bank or shelter to help out?"

Shaking his head, Felipe frowned. "No, unfortunately, you're going to see a lot of patients like her; kids who've lost their parents or even an entire family and live day to day, barely scraping by."

Pulling her stethoscope off her neck, she looked up at Felipe. "Can you ask her if it's okay if I give her a check-up, too? I promise

I'll get her the vitamins."

"¿Está bien que la doctora lo examine? ¿Y darte vitaminas?" He repeated the questions to the young child, who wore a rumpled tan tunic and bare feet.

Angel glanced up at Blaire and paused for a second before giving a confirmatory nod.

"Great." Blaire placed the stethoscope earpieces in her ears and lifted the bell to the child's chest. "I'm going to listen to your heart and lungs." She gave her a smile.

Ten minutes later, Blaire completed her exam. She'd listened to the girl's heart and lungs, looked in her ears and throat, and reviewed her height and weight on a growth chart. She made a clucking sound with her tongue and raised her eyes to meet Felipe's. "Tell her everything looks good, but I want to give her something else. Follow me."

He relayed her message to the child and waited for Blare to take the lead.

Moving around the exam table, now left empty after the girl hopped down, Blaire exited the room.

Angel and Felipe followed behind in silence. Once in the now-filled waiting area, Felipe told Blaire he'd get the next patient ready and meet her in the second exam room.

Blaire led Angel past the heart of the clinic to the kitchen in the back. The countertops were cleaned off, and all the evidence of breakfast cleared away. She rustled through a cupboard and found a loaf of bread and a jar of peanut butter. Pulling them out, she presented the offering to the child.

The little girl's eye's twinkled and a wide smile filled her face with joy and hope for the first time. "¿Para mi?" she asked, pointed at her chest.

Using context clues and dusting off her Spanish knowledge, Blaire assumed the girl had asked if she could have the items. Bobbing her head in agreement, Blaire stumbled through her response, "Si. Oh...y los vitaminas...I wish I had more to give you now, but I'll try to get extra food in the next few days. Oh, you probably don't know what I'm saying...well, I'll tell Felipe, and he can let you know—"

Angel had thrown her arms around Blaire, cutting off her rambling explanation.

What a sweet girl. Poor thing. Blaire stiffened, but thought it rude to interrupt the girl's outpouring of affection.

The girl released her embrace and seized the food out of Blaire's hands. She sent Blaire a grateful grin and scurried off.

"Don't forget your vitaminas!" Blaire shouted behind her, hoping Angel stopped at the medication table next to Juanita for her treasured supplements.

Wow. Blaire took so much for granted in her life. She didn't have to face hunger, poverty, or homelessness...well, that's not true. Technically, she was homeless. But not like this. Blaire had shoes and never went hungry. Realizing she'd only treated one patient and had a mountain of them left to see, she hurried to the exam rooms to join Felipe for her next visit.

Carrying on like this for the rest of the day, Blaire developed a rhythm with Felipe. By the end of the day, she'd seen at least forty patients. Blaire had dispensed vitamins, vaccines, and antiparasitic medications, and only experienced one mild panic attack after an elderly man hacked in her face. In her defense, he'd also spewed a greenish substance on her arm. She'd concealed her reaction until he left the room. Upon his exit, she'd gagged and scoured her arm with such vengeance it still remained red and raw.

As Blaire stood over the worn porcelain sink in the kitchen, scrubbing her arms for the umpteenth time, she wiped her forehead with her shirt sleeve to remove the sweat forming from the muggy day.

How would she last a whole month? The work felt rewarding...she thought back to the little girl from earlier in the morning, and her heart filled with warmth. But a month? Of heat and bugs and, well, generally being out of her comfort zone—by a mile. She could hear her mother clucking her tongue in her head. Blaire sighed.

"Why so down?"

Blaire jumped, startled by the unexpected interruption into her innermost thoughts. She turned around and saw the plump form of Juanita. Placing a hand to her chest, Blaire released the breath she'd been holding. "Whew. You scared me. I didn't hear you come in. How long have you been standing there?"

Juanita sent her a gentle smile and tilted her head as if to examine her new colleague. "Long enough to hear you muttering about bugs, Megan, your ability to make it here, and something about your mother."

Nodding, Blaire returned her attention to the sink and wrenched the faucet off. When the final trickle of water ceased, she lifted her head and set her eyes on Juanita again. She seemed to be a kind woman. Indeed, the town must think so, as every patient flocked to Juanita. They shared their medical concerns, town gossip, and baked goods. She listened to their questions, assisted those who couldn't walk well, and retrieved several cups of coffee for them.

Perhaps, Blaire could benefit from some of Juanita's wisdom. "Ahem. Uh…I guess I was…wondering how this next month would go, or if it would go at all." Blaire tore her gaze away from Juanita, focusing it instead on her own poor, reddened arms.

She rubbed her hand over the other forearm with a light touch. "I'm not sure I'm cut out for medicine at all, much less rural medicine or infectious disease. I don't speak the language well. And my mother only loves me if I'm perfect and thinks I've lost my mind coming here. She would like me to marry a senator and join the 'ladies who lunch.' Oh, and then there's Megan. My sister. Well, she was my sister. She's gone now." Blaire clamped her mouth shut, realizing she'd said too much.

Juanita took a step closer and laid a hand on Blaire's shoulder. "Gone? Like gone, gone?"

Tears brimmed near the surface, threatening to spill onto

Blaire's cheeks. She drew in a breath and held it for a moment before letting it out again. "Yeah. Like gone, gone. And there's nothing I can do about it. My parents always liked her better. 'The Golden Child,' that was Megan. Not me, though. I'm the black mark on the family. Nothing I do is ever good enough." Blaire blinked hard, and the tears she'd tried to hold back trailed down her face.

Patting her shoulder, Juanita spoke with a soft, soothing voice, "There, there. It's okay. I'm sure your parents love you. All parents love their children."

Sniffing, Blaire wiped her cheeks with the backs of her scoured hands. "Not mine."

"Nonsense. And you can't be a black mark on your family because you are a physician. They must be proud of that."

Blaire laughed at the inaccuracy of Juanita's statement. "Ha! That's what you think. No, my mother finds my work demeaning, below the Cunningham name. She would prefer I spend my time in philanthropy, cutting ribbons, donating their money to 'good' causes, and rubbing elbows with important people. But after Megan died…I wanted to make a difference. Megan passed away from meningitis, and I didn't want anyone else to suffer like she did. That's why I went into infectious disease."

Juanita reached out and lifted Blaire's chin, forcing Blaire to meet her eyes. "You are making a difference. I saw you with the patients today. You did a good job. They seem to take to you, and Angel couldn't stop singing your praises."

A slight smile tugged at the corner of Blaire's mouth but did not fully take residence. "Yeah, but I bet you noticed some other things, too."

"What other things?"

"It's okay. I know I do it—avoiding touching surfaces, the overuse of hand sanitizer and soap. I know I do it. I've tried to stop. I even went to therapy once, but…" Blaire shrugged.

Juanita raised a brow. "But what?"

"The therapist taught me a relaxation exercise and left the room for ten minutes…when she came back, she found me cleaning her chairs with wipes." Blaire gave a sheepish grin. "What can I say? I couldn't fully relax until I knew that the chair I was relaxing in wasn't contaminated."

Juanita belted out a hearty chuckle and slapped her thigh, causing the tassels at the bottom of the orange tunic underneath her white coat to shimmy. They matched her personality. Free and fun. "We've got to get you to lighten up. In time. It will happen. This place," she pointed to the ground, "this place, this town, this clinic, these people. They are special. They've been through a lot and survived. They'll teach you, too—how to live a new way. You'll see." And with that final piece of advice, Juanita patted Blaire on the shoulder and turned to leave.

"Juanita?"

Stopping, the tanned older woman paused and turned at the portico of the kitchen. She placed a hand on her hip and raised both brows. "Yes?"

"Thanks for listening…and please… don't mention any of this to Felipe. Especially the stuff about my family and Megan. I don't want him to think I can't make it here or that I'm weak. Okay?" Blaire asked, pleading with the woman to keep her secret.

Juanita stood still, but after a second, she shrugged. "Sure. I think you underestimate Felipe, but he won't hear any of this from me." Juanita glided away with this final pledge, humming a syncopated song, taking Blaire's secret with her.

It was the first time Blaire told anyone about Megan and her family other than Tiffany and Mabel. She expected to feel exposed and vulnerable, but instead, a lightness carried her up the stairs to her room. Something about Juanita was comforting, familiar even. Maybe she was right. This place may be exactly what she needed.

Chapter 18

"Buckle Up"

Blaire got ready for dinner, now refreshed after what her grandmother would have termed a "spit bath" using a full packet of skin-safe wipes. She'd changed clothes and brushed her hair. No way she was facing the electrocution shower again.

Just as she placed her hand on the knob to exit her room, Blaire's phone rang. She planned to leave her burgeoning bag behind and could see it vibrating on the floor, beckoning her attention. She walked over and rummaged through the bag, trying to answer the call before it went to voicemail. *Too late.* By the time her hands grasped the phone, its screen displayed the green symbol in the left corner, indicating a missed call. *Shoot. It was Tiffany.*

Blaire punched the home button to unlock the phone, and a text message came through. She pressed the window to read the message from her friend.

Hey girl, just checking on you. Hope you're settling in and (what I think was) your first day of clinic went well. Mabel and I've been praying for you… I'm sure you've already used your entire hand sanitizer supply by now. Lol. Seriously, try to enjoy the adventure and find joy in each day! Not everything has to be perfect. BTW, I ran into Darren at the mall yesterday. He asked how you were doing. I think he misses you, but good riddance—you can do better! Make sure to try new things. And DON'T eat that astronaut food. I know you snuck it into your bag. It's disgusting. Okay, talk to you soon. Oh, Mabel says she loves you, too. Bye.

Blaire laughed, rereading the text. Tiffany's voice danced in her head. She typed in a reply and pressed send, but nothing happened. Repeating the process resulted in the same frustrating end. Blaire scanned her phone and noted the battery had plenty of charge…but the service bars flicked between the words "No Service" and one sad, stunted bar. Sigh. Telling her friends about her day would have to wait. Maybe she could slip over to the internet café later.

She turned the phone off, tucking it away into her purse, and headed downstairs to dinner. Fingers crossed insects wouldn't make an appearance at the meal this time. She'd avoid the sugar bowl. Blaire grinned and walked through the archway to the kitchen. Her smile waned when her eyes fell upon Felipe sitting at the table, ready to dig into his meal.

Felipe both flustered and irritated her. Wearing a smirk as he watched her work throughout the day, she'd suspected he found her avoidance of germs and affinity for high heels and hand sanitizer entertaining.

An audible sigh escaped as Blaire walked to the counter and assembled her meal of a black soupy substance, a tortilla, and something resembling a large, nearly burnt, banana. Blaire lifted the plate to her nose and sniffed with caution. *It smelled…good. Hmm…*

Felipe watched the scene unfold and cleared his throat, interrupting her examination of the meal. "Uh, it's not going to bite. In fact, I'd wager this is the best food you'll eat in your life. Juanita made it, and most people in the community say she's the best cook around."

Scrunching her nose, Blaire walked to the table and took her seat, placing her plate before her. She pointed with her finger at the pooling dark puddle. "What's that?"

Felipe chuckled. "It's black beans. Homemade. Don't tell me you've never had black beans before?"

She shook her head. "We were more of a crudité and oyster Rockefeller family. So, no."

He sent her a half-smile. "Well, you won't see a lot of that fancy stuff around here."

She wasn't fancy…not really. Okay, yes, she liked things clean…but who didn't? Was that such a crime? Besides, he didn't know the first thing about her life and what she'd been through. How dare he pass judgment of her. Crossing her arms, she sent him a frown.

He didn't seem to notice her displeasure and continued with his education about the local cuisine. "We cook with what we grow on our farms; beans, corn, coffee. Even plantains." He nodded to the fruit on her plate.

"Oh, is that what this is? I wondered…I thought someone got mad at the banana and decided to destroy it with flames." She looked up and met Felipe's soulful eyes. Her pulse quickened, and heat rushed into her cheeks. She giggled at the thought of her oversized banana on fire.

He cracked a grin and chuckled. "Want to say grace? I'm starving."

"Sure." She tucked her head down and closed her eyes. "Dear God, thank You for this food, for unexpected adventures, and new friends. Amen." Blaire lifted her head, and she gave a small smile before picking up her fork. She poked at the beans and debated avoiding them altogether. Tiffany's voice resonated in Blaire's head, telling her to find joy in this experience, so she closed her eyes, took a bite, and swallowed. *Yum--it was good!*

Before she knew it, five minutes had passed in silence as she and Felipe cleaned their plates. With the final bite of charred plantain crossing her lips, she placed her fork down and dabbed her mouth with a napkin. "That was delicious. Seriously, some of the best food I've eaten. Ever. And I've been to the top restaurants in New York City."

She reached into the pocket of her black maxi skirt and pulled out a travel size bottle of sanitizer. She squeezed a small dab into the palm of one hand, clipped the lid closed, and tucked it away. The sharp scent of alcohol overshadowed the delicious fragrance of chili, onions, garlic, and pressed coffee.

Felipe nodded toward her pocket. "What's with that?"

She narrowed her eyes, bracing herself for the ridicule, which was sure to come. "What? It's sanitizer. Like we use in the clinic."

He stared at her, not saying anything.

"I mean...so, yes, I carry it with me everywhere, but lots of people do that. The world is a germy place, and I like to be prepared." She stopped speaking, realizing he still wore a blank look. "It's not a big deal...I just don't like...germs...or messes...or imperfections. What's wrong with that?"

Felipe opened his mouth but then shut it again as if debating how to respond. When he finally spoke, he did so with careful words, "There's nothing...wrong with wanting to keep things clean and to stay healthy, but..."

"But what?"

He reached his hand out and pulled it back before extending it once more and settling it on top of hers. Felipe looked into her eyes, crossing a threshold from colleagues to friends.

She didn't pull away from his touch.

"But life is...messy. And unpredictable. And fun. And perfectly imperfect. Maybe...I don't know...maybe relax a little." He smiled and moved his hand away, his face and neck reddening a bit.

"I'll try. You're not the first person to tell me that." She glanced at the digital clock on the microwave above the stovetop and yawned. 9:00 p.m. Blaire couldn't believe how tired she felt. She'd pulled countless overnight shifts at the hospital and felt more rested. Still, she supposed the trip's excitement and navigating her new world left her spent.

Rubbing her eyes, Blaire yawned again. "I better go to bed. I'm exhausted."

Felipe rose, too, and picked up their plates and cups from the table. He carried them to the sink and turned to her. "You go ahead. I'll clean up here."

She stretched her arms overhead. Relief washed over her. "Are you sure? I feel bad…"

He grinned and waved her away. "I'm sure. Besides, you have a big day tomorrow."

"Oh really? What's on the agenda?"

Felipe picked up the yellow sponge on the corner of the sink and squirted some blue dish detergent onto the stack of dishes. He turned on the nozzle and let the warm water create white pillows of soap in the middle of the pile. As he swirled the suds around, washing away the remnants of their meal, he shrugged. "Oh, you know. Heading out to the Finca. It's like a rural farm or ranch. There's a tight knit community of people there who either can't or won't travel here for care, so every few weeks we bring it to them."

Blaire bobbed her head in understanding. "Okay, sounds good." She started to leave the kitchen and go upstairs to crash for the night.

Felipe stopped her exit with a final warning, "Oh, and make sure you wear pants or shorts and sensible shoes. Something sturdy. Not like those heels you wore the first day. This farm is a good distance away, and the trip can be…demanding."

What did that mean? Demanding? But instead, she stuttered, "Okay. Good night," and scampered upstairs before he could dispense any more daunting news for the evening. She frowned.

How hard could the trek be? No worse than the ride on the big truck when she arrived. Hmm. Perhaps she should wear tennis shoes and tie her hair back tomorrow. Ooh, and pack extra hand soap, bug-spray, and wipes. Just in case.

Felipe's words rung in her ears, "Perfectly imperfect." Blaire knew only God, and His love was perfect, but it didn't stop her from striving for perfection. As if she could attain it on her own.

She swapped out her clothes for a soft, cotton white and pink floral pajama set. Sliding under her covers, Blaire pulled the quilt up to her chin. She eyed the corners of her room, searching for residual webs or their creators. Finding none, she flicked off her nightstand lamp, cloaking her room in darkness.

Still not reassured about her sleeping quarters' safety from insects, she pulled her bed coverings all the way over her face. She was *not* letting any bugs near her mouth. Closing her eyes, she wondered if maybe Tiffany and Felipe were right. Perhaps she did need to loosen up and let go of her fear.

Blaire tugged the sheet down to let her face peek above it but immediately retreated into the safety of her cotton-clad tent. Maybe she'd loosen up tomorrow. Blaire whispered a prayer for God to help her trust Him...to relax, even a little. And with this final thought, she closed her eyes and fell into a muggy, but safe sleep.

Chapter 19

"It's Going to Be a Bumpy Ride"

Felipe tightened the tattered and worn yellow strap holding multiple backpacks in his battered truck's bed. He'd finally gotten it repaired, but the exterior screamed for attention. Nevertheless, when he'd tried the ignition earlier that morning, it had purred, promising to whisk him and Blaire to the farm over two hours away. He hoped

As he secured the final strap in place, he heard footsteps approach. He turned around, and his jaw dropped. Dr. Cunningham stood before him wearing the most inappropriate outfit for the upcoming journey, but she looked gorgeous. She had heeded his footwear advice, as he noted the flat black shoes on her feet. That must have been the only suggestion she'd heeded because a flowing, red skirt and fitted black top encased her tempting curves. The hot Guatemalan sun kissed the tip of her nose and cheeks, bringing out a faint dusting of freckles. A few lighter strands of hair tinted copper by the sunlight warmed her peaches and cream complexion.

Blaire stood still, watching his appraisal and waiting for a commentary. "Well?" She wiggled her foot, showing him her shoes. "I wore flats." Planting her hands on her hips, she beamed.

Shaking his head, a broad grin formed on Felipe's lips. "Yeah. I see that." He nodded toward the cab of the truck. "Hop in. We'd better get going, or we're going to be late. It's a long haul to get there."

She walked around to the truck's passenger side, opened the door, and climbed in with obvious difficulty.

Guilt washed over Felipe. He should have opened the door for her, but he wasn't thinking straight. She made his head swim, and he hadn't been in a serious relationship before or even spent time with women his own age. Much less women as beautiful and intelligent as Dr. Cunningham. Even if she had an uncanny affinity for cleaning products.

He started to smile, but then realized he'd been staring at her the entire time and tried to snap himself out of his inner monologue. Felipe whistled and his long-time confidant and pal, Pedro, came running. He clamored into the cab and nestled into his spot between Felipe and Blaire.

Blaire frowned. "He's a mess."

"He's not a mess. He's a dog. Dogs are supposed to get dirty when they run and play outside." Felipe covered the canine's ears with his hands. "Don't say it too loudly, you'll hurt his feelings."

Confirming this truth, the animal lifted his head and cast an injured look to Blaire before planting his head on top of his paws.

"Sorry, I should've helped you get in the truck. It's kind of high."

She gave him a smile and waved his offer away. "It's fine. I'm a city girl, remember? I can take care of myself." Blaire gestured with her thumb to the truck bed. "What's in the back?"

Felipe placed the key in the ignition but paused before turning it. He glanced over, assessing his colleague. "Supplies. Medical equipment, antibiotics, vitamins, other medications. Just the usual." She really was pretty, although he didn't know how her skirt would hold up on the back of a horse. "Oh, and I brought you a quilt."

She scrunched her nose. "A quilt? It's a million degrees out here. What in the world do I need a quilt for today?"

He turned the key and grinned, not meeting her gaze. "The horse. Thought you might need a cushion. Figured you didn't do a lot of horseback riding back home in New York City. Am I wrong?" He peered at her through the side of his eye.

"A horse. A horse? Why are we riding a horse? We're taking a truck." A look of mild panic painted itself across her face.

Felipe headed down the dirt path that led away from the clinic, kicking dust along the way. "The truck is just to get us through the first leg of our trip. It's about a two-hour drive to the main ranch. The temporary clinic is another twenty to thirty-minute ride by horseback from there. The trail is too narrow for the truck. Plus, sometimes rainfall makes the road so mucky the tires would get stuck. And that's if the bushes and trees on the side didn't take us out first. So, horseback it is." He tossed her a glance for a brief second before returning his focus to the road. "So, was I wrong? Or are you secretly a great equestrian?

Wringing her hands in her lap, Blaire stammered, "Uh—uh, no. No, I'm not a great equestrian. I'm not any kind of equestrian, thank you very much. I wish you'd warned me about the horse."

He noticed her eyeing her skirt. "Yeah, I told you to dress appropriately."

Blaire smacked her thighs, grasping at the skirt. "This is appropriate, just not for a long horseback ride." She blew out a long breath and then gasped. "Are these horses clean?"

A belly laugh erupted from deep within Felipe. This girl was hilarious. A real trip. Who asks if the horse is clean? It lives in a barn and runs around in dirt and dust. Sure, his friend, who lent Felipe the horses, took excellent care of them.

Felipe supposed they got the standard number of brushings, baths, shoe fittings, and feeds required to maintain good health. But come on. They were horses. He nodded. "Yeah...they're clean."

He rode in silence for the remainder of the trip and wondered what went through Blaire's mind when she signed up to volunteer at his clinic. She didn't seem prepared, and she didn't fit in the clinic or community. Not to mention her fear of germs and dirt. How would they work together for the next month?

As he pondered all of this, Felipe felt God tugging at his heart, reminding him to be thankful for the help; any help. He sent a whisper of thanks to the heavens and pulled into the one level ranch-style building. A large stable with two horses tied to a wooden pole sat next to it.

Felipe turned off the truck and turned to Blaire. "Phase One; Complete. Hop out. Ready for phase two?" He grinned, ambled out of the cab, and shut the door. He stood six feet ahead of her by the time she opened her door and stepped out. "What about the dog? We can't leave him here in the heat?"

He whistled for his pal, who perked up his head at the familiar sound and bounded out of Blaire's open door, nearly knocking her over in the process.

"Don't mind me," she grumbled under breath.

"What was that?"

Blaire shook her head. "Nothing. I'm good. Is the dog going to ride on horseback with you?"

Was she serious? Felipe burst into uncontained laughter at the ridiculous thought of his dog on the back of the saddle with him. After he regained his composure, he replied, "No. He'll stay here in the barn where it's shaded and wait for us to pick him up on the way home.

The dog jogged to the sheltered side of the barn and plopped down. He stretched his legs out and yawned. He popped open one eye to check on Felipe and sent Blaire one last warning glance before closing it and drifting off to sleep.

Felipe walked up to the larger horse, a brute of an animal standing at least six feet tall. He came to the top of Felipe's head. His chestnut brown coat glistened in the sun, and he swatted his tail at the horseflies encroaching him. Grabbing the bridle, Felipe patted the horse's head, saying a few words in a soft voice. Pulling an apple out of his pocket, Felipe fed it to the animal. The horse nuzzled it out of his hand and stomped his foot with pleasure.

He waved Blaire over. "Come on. I'll help you up and grab my bags, and we'll hit the trail."

She sent him a tentative smile and then joined him next to her ride. Blaire stopped next to the horse, which, although a half a foot shorter than Felipe's, still stood a few inches above her five-foot two-inch frame. She reached a trembling hand toward the horse and paused before placing it on her ride.

Felipe nodded. "It's okay. You can pet her. Introduce yourself."

"Hi there. Uh, I'm Blaire." She placed her hand on the middle of the creature's back. After a few cautious strokes, her shoulders relaxed, and a small smile tugged at her lips. The horse whinnied, and Blaire jumped, clutching her chest. "Oh, my. She scared me."

Chuckling, Felipe dug in his pocket and handed over another piece of apple for Blaire to share with her new friend. He grabbed her hand without thinking and placed the fruit in her palm. "Keep your hand flat, like this." He demonstrated with his free hand. "That way, she can get a piece without taking a bit of your finger with it."

She furrowed her brow.

"I'm kidding. Sort of. She won't bite you, at least not on purpose. She's about the most mild-mannered horse around."

The horse nibbled on Blaire's offering and nodded his head in approval.

Felipe reached a hand to her and raised a brow. "Ready to get on?"

Swallowing hard, Blaire closed her eyes for a moment. Her lips settled into a thin line, but when she opened them, she nodded in confirmation. "Okay. Ready."

There was a saddle in place on the center of the horse's back, nestled on a small blanket. Felipe jogged to the truck and grabbed the backpacks and the extra padded blanket. He placed it on top of Blaire's saddle and pulled the belt buckle on the underside tight.

One more tug and Felipe was pleased with his work. "Okay. Come stand in front of the saddle.

Blaire complied with his request, walking over to stand next to the horse and Felipe.

He stepped closer, brushing Blaire's back with his chest. Felipe guided her left hand to the saddle. Place your left hand on the horn--that's the knobby thing--up here at the front."

Felipe continued with his instruction, "Good. Now take your right hand and grip the back of the saddle. And hold tight."

Standing so close to Blaire made him wonder what it would be like to hold her in his arms. He drew in a deep breath, inhaling the sweet scent of lilac from her perfume or shampoo. *Pay attention. She's a colleague, and she's leaving in a few weeks.* He shook his head.

"Then, place your left foot in the stirrup down here." He pointed to the swinging piece of metal attached to the saddle. "And when you step into it, hold tight to the horn and back of the saddle and hoist your right leg over the seat."

She shoved her foot in the stirrup and gripped the saddle tighter. Counting aloud, she uttered, "One, two, three," and swung her right leg across the middle of the horse. Once she landed as planned, bottom in the seat, facing forward with all limbs intact, she rewarded Felipe with a gorgeous, broad grin. "I did it!"

He nodded his head, sending her a half-smile. "Yep, you sure did." He untied the reins from the wooden post and handed them over the horse's head to her. "Hold them in one hand like this," he placed them in her left hand, wrapping his strong, rough fingers over the delicate, pale skin of hers. The softness of her touch sent a jolt through him and made his heart bolt into action, much like the horse looked like she wanted to do.

Realizing if he didn't want to send Blaire on a wild ride, then he better pay attention. Felipe pulled his hand back from hers quickly and pointed at the saddle horn. "If you feel unsteady, then you can grab on to this. It won't make you look like a true horseman, or horsewoman, I guess, but it'll help keep you on top. Especially if Armoniá decides to make a run for it."

Fear flashed across her face, and Blaire gripped the horn until her knuckles turned white. "Who's Armoniá?"

Felipe gestured to the horse holding Blaire's weight. "Your ride."

"Oh, right. Of course. Just one more question. Well, actually make that two." Her grip tightened.

Felipe walked around the front of Blaire's steed and untied the reins for his ride, a taller horse named Thunder. He placed the reins over the front of the horse with care, grabbed his saddle, and heaved himself into his seat with one fluid motion. He lifted his eyes to Blaire's. "Fire away."

"Uh, okay…why would…uh…Armoniá here, why would he—"

"She."

"Right, she, why would she decide to 'make a run for it' as you said?"

"Well, she's a reliable animal, but if something startled her like a bird, or maybe a snake—"

Blaire gasped, and her hand flew to her mouth. "Snakes? You didn't say anything about snakes."

Felipe put one palm in the air in a "calm down" fashion and attempted to soothe her. They'd never make it to the clinic before midnight at this rate. "I'm not saying there will be a snake. I'm just using it as an example. Please, don't worry. Now, what's the other question?"

She peered at him through narrowed eyes, a look of distrust forming on her face. "How do I make him, I mean, her, stop. Where are the breaks?" She scrunched her face, obviously perplexed.

Now sitting atop Thunder, Felipe doubled over, laughing at the absurdity of her request. When he righted himself again, he lifted his eyes to hers and could almost feel the flames of anger shooting out from them. Even so, he still suspected he could lose himself in those eyes if he tried.

Something about Dr. Cunningham pulled at his heart. He had never met anyone like her before. She infuriated him at times…but her beauty and brains captivated him. He found the flush of crimson filling her cheeks from her anger at his response exhilarating.

Her scowl deepened.

He raised both hands and his reins. "I'm sorry. I'm not making fun of you…not really. I've just never seen someone approach a horse like a car before, that's all."

"Glad I could provide entertainment for the day."

Felipe turned Thunder's head to the right, guiding him away from the fence post and toward the trailhead. "Awe, it's not like that. Now, back to those breaks. If you want to stop, pull back with a firm grip on the reins. Easy, but firm. Try not to jerk on them. They don't like that—the horses, not the reins."

Staring at the two foreign pieces of leather in front of her, Blaire gave a slight nod of her head but sat frozen atop her horse. "Do I tell the horse to follow you? How do I get it to move?"

"Just give her a little nudge with your heels, easy though, and then pull the reins to the right, and she'll know what to do. She's a pro."

Blaire obliged and rewarded him with a wide smile. Lifting her head, she said, "Now what?"

"Now, we ride. Give her a click of your tongue, like this," Felipe made a kissing sound, and his horse picked up the pace to a slow trot, "and stay behind me."

She followed his lead and settled into a rhythm behind him.

Felipe rode in silence for five or ten minutes until he heard Blaire's small voice pierce the solitude.

"Do you mind my asking how long it's going to take for us to get there?"

He continued forward, not looking back. "Why? Do you have somewhere else you need to be?"

Although the narrow trail created an unpleasant cloud with every clip-clop of the horses' hooves, the surrounding tree's shade kept the blistering heat at bay. "No, but my backside is getting sore, there's dust in my eyes, and I think about a million flies have bitten me in the past ten minutes." As if to prove her point, she smacked at another critter on her upper left arm with her free hand.

Felipe didn't turn around. "Well, I hate to tell you this, but you've got about a trillion more bites to go because our destination is another thirty to forty minutes away. That's why we're going to them. It's too much of a haul for most villagers to come to our clinic." He heard a smack as undoubtedly another flying insect met its demise at Blaire's hand.

"It's fine. I don't like bugs. I'm sure you've noticed. To be honest, I don't like bugs, dirt, germs, or anything that could make you sick. But I especially have a thing about mosquitos. Now I'm rambling," Blaire stopped speaking as abruptly as she'd started.

Felipe peered over his right shoulder and raised one brow. "What's the deal with the mosquito vendetta? Not that I love getting bit myself."

She frowned, and her eyes darkened. "My sister…my sister died from meningitis during her first year of college. The doctors weren't sure about the source of the infection, but she'd gone on a spring break trip, and they suspected it came from a mosquito bite." She fell silent again and offered no further explanation.

Pulling back on his reins, Felipe stopped his horse and turned his upper body around.

Blaire fixed her gaze on her reins, but stopped, too.

"Hey." He waited until she lifted her eyes to his. "Hey, I'm sorry. I'm sorry about your sister…I didn't realize."

A thin layer of tears glistened in her eyes, and Blaire paused before speaking, "No. No, how could you know? It's okay. Well, it's not okay, but it's not your fault she's gone. That's why I'm the way I am. Or at least I think that's why I'm the way I am--with the wipes and the cleaning and everything. I even went into infectious disease to try to make up for what happened to her. Thought it would make my parents proud, too. But that's a whole other story." She wiped away a single tear from her cheek before replacing her vulnerable countenance with her usual guarded mask. "So, what are we waiting for? We've got patients expecting us."

Felipe searched her beautiful face for a crack in the façade, but finding none, returned his focus to the trail ahead, leading to the full clinic awaiting them.

He considered stopping and insisting she tell him more about her sister and her family, but the moment had passed. No, she made it clear that she didn't want to talk about it, at least not with him. He had to respect that. Besides, Blaire—no, Dr. Cunningham—was only here for a few more weeks. A few more weeks—the thought unsettled him. Why did he care? He squeezed his heels, causing the horse to trot and carry him away from his conversation with the doctor and his increasingly perplexing feelings about her.

Chapter 20

"Laughter Is the Best Medicine"

When her horse came to a full stop, Blaire exhaled the breath she didn't realize she'd held the entire ride. Forty minutes on horseback. More like four hundred. She had the bites and bruises to prove it. She was confident her backside looked like the eye of a heavyweight boxer after nine rounds in a Friday night fight. She swung her right leg over the top of the saddle, holding on for her life as she attempted a graceful dismount. It was not meant to be. Thud. Make that ten rounds in the fight-her backside took another hit.

His muscular arms glistened with sweat. He stretched them to Blaire, an apologetic grin on his face. "Sorry about that. I should've helped you down."

She took his hands, and once righted again, Blaire brushed at the dust, turning her clothing a lighter shade. After she'd removed as much of it as possible, she lifted her head. Wow. His dark eyes drew her in, and she liked how the humidity caused his short, wavy hair to curl.

One rogue piece swooped across his forehead, causing him to run a hand through it to get it out of his way.

Her knees weakened, and she cleared her throat to distract herself. "Ahem, so…what now? Where do we put the horses? Where's the clinic set up? What's the plan?" She rattled off a series of questions.

Felipe took the reins from her and handed both horses off to a shorter man. The man wore a red flannel shirt and overalls despite the sweltering heat, and his knuckles and fingers curved from years of arthritic change.

The man, whom Blaire guessed to be in his eighties, sent her a slow smile and a tip of his head. He walked away in silence with a rein in each hand and both horses in tow. The beasts must have respected the man because they followed without making a snort or stomp.

Smoothing out her skirt, Blaire took a step toward Felipe. She nodded toward the back of the retreating man. "He doesn't say much, does he?"

"Nope. Now, we better get going." He looked at the worn, black, and canvas wristwatch on his left arm. "We're late."

Bringing up the topic of Megan earlier left Blaire unsettled. She missed her older sister terribly. Her passing left a hole in Blaire's heart, not to be filled by anyone else. She wished Megan could see her now--riding horseback (in a skirt, no less), getting dusty, letting her hair down, albeit now frizzy. Blaire smiled at the thought.

Megan would have joined Blaire on the adventure and sprinkled her joy and lightness around like glitter. Blaire prayed for one more chance to talk to her, one more moment to hold her hand. She longed to hug her sister and ask her how to handle their parents. How to handle life.

A sigh escaped her lips. Best tuck away those thoughts as they'd only lead to more tears.

Felipe must have noticed her delay because he'd stopped his advance to the small cement building. He turned around and nodded toward the building. "You coming?"

She pulled in a breath and released it along with her sad thoughts. "Yep. I'm coming." She was determined to make it through the month. She had a lot to prove to Felipe, Dr. Sedgewick, and herself.

Lost in her thoughts, Blaire barely noticed a small child no older than three or four, tugging at her hand. The little boy stood three feet high and appeared unkempt. A smear of dirt across his forehead and his rumpled clothes made it appear neither items had been scrubbed in weeks. She glanced down and noted his bare feet covered in muck from the dark, mushy soil.

He yanked again, and Blaire, entranced by the child, forgot about her germaphobic ways at his soft touch. He guided her by the hand, insisting in silence that she follow him.

Blaire pulled her eyes away from the boy for a moment, scanning the trail ahead for Felipe, but he was not in sight. Deciding to go with her young new friend, she obliged and trudged behind him.

The child stopped at the edge of the village underneath a towering tree. It had a thick, multicolored trunk made of orange and neon green stripes as if someone had passed by and painted it with delightful, uninhibited strokes. Its lush green leaves provided a welcome canopy and the only shade around for hundreds of feet.

Below the tree sat an elderly woman with a silver braid down to her waist. She wore a tattered beige dress pulled up to her knees, her bare feet on the ground. She rested her back against the beautiful trunk, tilting her head up to the sky. Her eyes remained closed, but her mouth hung open as if she couldn't gather enough air. Beads of perspiration pooled on her forehead and her sallow face contrasted against her otherwise tanned skin.

The boy pulled on Blaire's hand once more, demanding her attention. He pointed toward the older woman beneath the tree and sat down next to her.

Oh. Perhaps this was the boy's grandmother? She didn't look well. Blaire peered over her shoulder, hoping to find someone to help or at least translate. *Where was Felipe?* Blaire sighed. She was on her own.

Dusting off her rusty knowledge from Spanish class eons ago, Blaire spoke in broken, poorly accented phrases, "Hola…Yo soy La Doctora Cunningham. Uh…¿está bien?"

The older woman opened her eyes and scanned Blaire's face. She gave her a small measured shake of the head before closing her eyes again and returning her head to its previous position.

No, of course, she's not okay. Otherwise, she wouldn't be sitting under this tree. Way to go, Blaire. "¿Uh…tiene… (what was the word for pain?) dolor?"

Her patient didn't move her head this time but instead pointed to her chest.

Chest pain. And in this heat…far away from a hospital. Not good. Blaire had slung a bright red medical bag over her shoulder. She unzipped it, bypassed the wipes and sanitizer, and pulled out her stethoscope. Placing the earpieces in position, Blaire lifted the stethoscope's bell to the woman's chest. After a few minutes of listening, she'd discovered the woman's heart rhythm sounded regular, her rate was fine, but her lungs wheezed. She turned to the woman. "Tiene asma?"

The woman gave her a blank stare.

Hmm, maybe she'd said it wrong? Or perhaps they called it something else here? She tried again, "¿Tiene…un inhalador?"

The little boy's eyes widened. He nodded his head with vigor and made a gesture with his hand to his mouth, simulating an inhaler.

Blaire raised her brow. "Where is it…I mean, dónde?" She groped around her medical bag again, hoping she'd packed one. Lifting her head, she surveyed the woman again. Did her color look worse?

The woman gave a slight shrug of the shoulders, indicating her inhaler's whereabouts were a mystery.

Come on, Blaire. It's got to be in here. Aha! Her fingers closed around the treasured object. She yanked it out and thrust it to the woman's lips. "Here, here. Take a deep breath. I mean, respiración. Por favor."

Her patient placed her lips around the hub of the red inhaler and drew in a deep breath as Blaire pressed the canister and sent a puff of the medication into the woman's lungs.

Blaire leaned in, one hand behind the woman's head and the other one still holding the inhaler for her. "One more time. Uh…una más. Please."

Blaire didn't know if the woman trusted her or not, but she repeated the process, taking another long draw off the container.

Within a few minutes, the woman's shoulders relaxed, and her cheeks flushed a pink color. *Much better.*

Footsteps approached from behind Blaire. She peeked to see who was coming, still keeping a hand on her patient. *Felipe.* "Hey. Where've you been?"

Felipe kneeled next to Blaire's side, so close his arm brushed against hers. He took in the scene before him. "I'm sorry. I shouldn't have left you back there. I turned around, and you'd gone. I walked in a big circle around the village, and finally, another patient mentioned they'd seen you head this way. Is she okay?" He tilted his head toward the patient and frowned.

Blaire locked eyes with Felipe, and his caring eyes provided a safe refuge. "Yeah, she is now. She was having an asthma attack, and she didn't have an inhaler." Blaire pointed at her loud-colored satchel. "I'm always prepared." She patted the bag. "My Spanish is not as great as it used to be, but we managed." She turned to the little boy and tried to recall how to ask him his name. "¿Cómo te llamas?"

A faint, small voice replied, "Rico." He gave her a rewarding grin, revealing dimples in both cheeks.

Blaire gave her patient's lungs another listen. This time she found good air movement and no wheezing. Whew. *The woman was going to be okay.*

"May I?" Felipe nudged her, asking permission to translate.

"Sure. That'd be great."

Felipe spoke in rapid Spanish. Though Blaire picked up an occasional "how" and "when," a lot of the conversation blew over her head. By the time he finished his conversation with the older woman, the little boy had climbed into her lap.

Felipe stood up and placed two fingers to his lips. He gave a loud whistle, and two other men wearing brown overalls, and beige t-shirts jogged over.

One of the men carried a large water bottle with him and passed it to the older woman.

After she took a long drink, she opened her eyes and smiled at Blaire.

Blaire returned the grin and rose, joining Felipe.

"Gracias," was all the woman said as the two men helped lift her to a standing position and guided her back to the main building.

Waving goodbye to the lady and her grandchild filled Blaire with warmth.

"It feels good, doesn't it?"

She looked over at Felipe and couldn't ignore how handsome he was, rolling his sleeves up and revealing his well-formed forearms. Self-conscious, she placed a palm to her cheek, patting at the stickiness from the heat on her skin. "What?"

"Helping out. Helping people who really need it, who wouldn't get the help if you weren't here. It feels good." He leaned in closer, his eyes searching her face.

"Yeah, it does. Is that why you do it?"

He shook his head. "No. I mean, it is, but that's not all of it…"

Blaire shrugged. "So, why else do it?" Dusting off the remnants of debris from her skirt, she waited for his answer.

"That's another story for another time. A long story." He glanced at his watch. "Come on. I saw a line forming at the clinic. We're both in for a long day." He reached out his hand to her. "By the way, the lady's name was Virginia, and she said you had a kind heart. She also said she thought you fit in well here."

Blaire accepted his hand, unsure of why or how she was holding his, but happy about it, nonetheless. "That was nice of her. But I was just doing my job." She walked in silence to the small satellite clinic, realizing that she hadn't thought once about her hand sanitizer and wipes for the first time since bending down to help Virginia. She'd been so concerned about the woman and the little boy; it had slipped her mind. Huh…maybe Virginia was right…maybe she was starting to fit in."

Chapter 21

"Take the Saddle by the Horn"

Blaire wiped the perspiration off her clammy forehead with the back of her hand and scanned the room. She'd completed her fortieth visit of the day—that's not true, forty-first if she counted the elderly woman under the tree at the beginning of the day. "It looks like that was the last one."

Felipe surveyed the waiting area and nodded. "Yep. I think we're done." He pulled a black handkerchief out of his pocket. He wiped it across his neck before standing up from his seat and placing bottles of vitamins and medication into the duffle bags he'd brought from La Clinica.

Removing her stethoscope from her neck, Blaire tucked it away into her red bag and started cleaning her area, too. "Great. It was a good day, but I'm beat. And sweaty." She snuck a squirt of hand sanitizer and tucked her last items away.

"You ready to head out?" Felipe zipped his bags and picked them up to carry them to their ride.

She had hoped to say goodbye to the little boy, Rico, and his grandmother from earlier, but glancing around the empty room told her they'd left for the day.

Rolling his sleeves up further, Felipe stepped closer, closing the gap between the two of them. "Looking for someone?"

Her pulse quickened, and she sent him a shake of the head. "No. Well, I was going to say goodbye to Rico, but I guess he and his grandmother left." Blaire didn't know why Felipe made her so nervous, but the fact remained that he did. Despite knowing him for a brief time, she found herself sharing pieces of herself she'd hidden away from the world.

"I guess they made an impact on you, huh? That's the thing about coming here to work. These people leave an imprint on you. They leave a mark--a kind of tattoo on your heart." Felipe tilted his head toward the ranch hand, holding their horses nearby, indicating she should follow him. "Maybe we'll make another trip out here in a few weeks before you leave." He made a sharp turn on his heel and strode toward the ranch hand.

"Right...before I leave." She'd forgotten her time was so limited and fleeting here. When she first made plans to come to Guatemala, she'd been less than enthusiastic. But now...she didn't know. Something had changed. Not that she didn't still want to pursue her infectious disease fellowship...that had been the plan since Megan passed. But now, between talks with Juanita and her time at the clinic and the Finca with Felipe...well, she'd be lying if she said she wouldn't miss it...at least a little.

Felipe turned around and saw Blaire had stopped walking. She stood frozen and still as a statue. "Well? Come on. You don't want to be riding to the truck when the sun sets. Not the best idea to be in the wild at night. There's pumas, jaguars, snakes...even crocodiles out here."

"Jaguars?!" Blaire bolted from her statuesque pose and

scampered to her ride for the evening.

Armoniá eyed Blaire up and down and gave a low, unimpressed whinny.

Funny, that's how Blaire felt about her reacquaintance with her horse, too. She snickered.

Felipe approached her with one duffle bag still in hand, and the other slung across his chest. He set the bag in his hand down on the ground and extended a hand of help to Blaire. "What's so funny?"

She attempted to heave herself onto her stead unassisted, but after two or three failed attempts, she sighed and accepted Felipe's hand. He boosted her atop the horse, and she landed with a thud. "Oh, nothing. Just thinking that Armoniá and I are both experiencing the same level of excitement about our reunion."

Armoniá stomped a foot and swayed her head up and down, agreeing with Blaire.

Blaire waited for Felipe to hop on Thunder and settle into place. Taking the reins in his hands, he guided the horse away from the post and toward the narrow trailhead to begin the journey home to La Clinica. He peered over his shoulder. "You good?"

She sucked in a deep breath and tightened her grip on the weathered brown reins. Raising her head, she sent him a curt nod. "Yep. At least I think so.... I hope so," she muttered the last phrase under her breath.

Armoniá took the lead and fell into step behind Felipe's horse, and the two of them clip-clopped along in silence for at least ten minutes.

The rocking motion of the horse's gait lulled Blaire into a trance, and her thoughts drifted to the older woman and her grandson. It had felt good to help them. Like the reason, she went into medicine in the first place.

She wondered if Dr. Sedgewick would really take her back into the Infectious Disease program and if he said yes if she still wanted to go. Of course, she did. That had been the plan for years. Become an infectious disease physician, redeem the loss of Megan, and prove to her parents that she, Blaire Cunningham, could be the daughter they'd always wanted.

Turning these thoughts over in her mind, Blaire didn't notice the dark storm clouds gathering overhead. A few water droplets fell from the sky and landed on her nose, jostling her out of her rumination.

She tipped her head toward the heavens, and more drops pelted her face. "Hey, it's raining."

Felipe didn't stop or turn around but instead continued moving forward. "Yep, sure is."

After a few more clip-clops, Blaire's voice broke the silence again, "So?"

"So what? Are you going to melt?"

Blaire furrowed her brow and grunted. "Haha. No, I'm not going to melt, thank you very much. I meant it's raining. Is it okay to have the horses out in the rain? Is it safe to ride in the rain? This is my first trail ride, you know."

Remaining stoic, Felipe lumbered along atop Thunder. "Sure, it's okay. They're animals and used to the physical elements to some extent. They can probably navigate the muddy terrain better than you can on foot."

A few minutes passed, and the droplets transformed into sprinkles and then a full-on downpour. The heavy rainfall obscured Blaire's vision, making it difficult to see beyond Armoniá's head, much less Felipe up ahead. Blaire cupped her hands around her mouth and shouted, "It's getting pretty bad out here. I can hardly see you."

Getting no response, she tightened her grip on the reins with one hand and attempted to wipe the swath of wetness out of her eyes with the other one. *This was not good.*

Armoniá must have concurred because she whinnied and shook her head, pulling on the reins.

A low warning rumble of thunder sounded, and the hairs on Blaire's arms rose. No, she did not like this one bit. She shivered and squinted her eyes, begging a glimpse of Felipe's silhouette. She squeezed her legs, applying encouraging pressure to her horse's flanks.

Armoniá picked up the pace to a slight trot. Instead of the smooth and steady ride, Blaire had experienced earlier in the day, this gait felt stilted and skittish.

As Blaire contemplated her options and readied her hands to shout again, a bolt of lightning struck a tree behind her, making a brilliant flash of light and a deafening crack. She jerked her upper body around and visualized the now-fallen tree lying charred and broken on the ground.

Armoniá reared up on her hind legs and whinnied.

No, no, no. This was not happening. Leaning forward, Blaire clutched the horse's neck, holding the reins and digging her fingers into her mane. Don't let go. Whatever happens, don't let go.

The horse's feet landed upon the ground, and Blaire exhaled, thankful to be horizontal once again. Her relief was short-lived. As soon as her hooves hit the mucky earth, Armoniá tore off at a gallop.

The horse blew past what Blaire assumed was Felipe and Thunder, although she couldn't be confident between the rain and her blinding fear.

Blaire thought she heard Felipe's voice shouting instructions at her, but all she could focus on at the present time was not falling off and maiming herself or dying.

Blaire tucked her head down, holding on with everything she possessed. She pulled her legs in and screamed, "Help! Help! You silly horse, stop, stop. I said, stop it. Help!" *God, please make this horse stop. I promise if you get me off of this animal in one piece, I will do anything. I'll relax. I'll quit sanitizing everything. I'll even stay and work at the clinic if you just let me live. Please.*

With her final plea, Blaire heard a man's voice behind her. As she considered the physical ramifications of her impending riding accident, a hand reached across her and grabbed the reins.

After a quick, firm yank on the reins, Armoniá came to an abrupt stop.

Inertia is a funny thing…Blaire recalled learning about it during her first physics class. Every action has an equal and opposite reaction. Unfortunately, the equal and opposite reaction to her stead stopping on a dime was Blaire's body hurtling over her horse's head. She landed in a belly flop, face down in the mud below. "Oof," she groaned.

A pair of boots trudged up next to her head. "Hey, are you okay, Blaire?"

Was she okay? She took a mental inventory. *Let's see…head…still attached…arms and legs…moveable although her left ankle hurt.* She wiggled her fingers and toes. *Yep, those functioned.*

She placed her hands under her chest in a push-up position and heaved herself upward. Oh no. She'd fallen off a horse. She'd fallen off a horse! *How in the world had this happened?* She blamed the rain, and the thunder, and her general affinity for disasters. Plus, she figured God must have a sense of humor…what with causing a germaphobe to land face first in sludge.

Felipe reached down and placed a hand on her shoulder. "Did you hear me?"

She swiped away a film of mud from her eyelids with her thumb so she could see her concerned hero better. Blaire nodded slowly. "Yeah, I-I think so. At least…I don't think anything is broken, but…my ankle hurts. I don't know if I can walk on it."

Scooting closer to examine her foot, Felipe frowned. "Let me take a look." He gently placed his hands on either side of her ankle and raised his head, sending her a smile.

She leaned back on her hands and winced. "Okay." The touch of his hand on her skin sent a tingle through her. Butterflies flitted around in her stomach at his compassionate smile.

Blaire placed a hand to her cheek. She must look terrible. It seemed she was coated from head to toe in a complete layer of filth.

After a few minutes of pressing on some bones and turning her foot in different directions in a cautious manner, Felipe lifted his head. "I don't think it's broken, either, but you've got a pretty good sprain. I bet it's black and blue in the morning." He shifted toward her head and reached his hand outward. "Here, put your arm around my shoulders. I'm going to lift you up and try to get you on my horse with me."

Felipe encircled one arm around her shoulders and another under her legs. He lifted her into his arms and stood up one foot at a time, careful not to jostle her. After setting her in the front of the saddle, he took his place behind her. Wrapping his strong arms around her, Felipe made her feel safe. He grasped the reins in front of her.

"Come on, Thunder. Let's get this pretty lady home." He clicked his tongue, signaling to the horse to go.

Blaire put a gentle hand on his forearm, trying to stop him from leaving. She turned her head and peered over her shoulder. "Wait...what about Armoniá? We can't leave her here?"

"Don't worry. She's coming with us. Armoniá's a reliable trail horse, and that means she knows to follow the leader. As soon as we leave, she'll fall in line behind us. Trust me. I'd never leave her behind."

Blaire liked that he was concerned about the horse...and her. And she couldn't ignore that he'd called her pretty.

The rain faded to a faint drizzle, and Blaire had managed to wipe most of the mud off her face. She turned further, locking eyes with Felipe, and her heart pounded in her chest. For a brief moment, she thought he might kiss her, and she leaned in, closing her eyes. A final lightning crash startled her and caused her eyes to fly wide open again.

She whipped around, sure that the horses might bolt at the sound, but Felipe spoke soothing words to them. Felipe's horse side-stepped and skirted about for a minute or two, but he didn't take off.

Felipe pulled on the reins, urging the horse to stay still. He caught Blaire's gaze. "We better go...it's getting late. You good?"

Staring into his eyes as they stood still, Blaire whispered, "Yeah,

I'm good." It was not completely the truth as her left ankle throbbed. She suspected it would be three times its normal size by morning. Sitting so close to Felipe with his arms wrapped around her, she didn't care.

With another tongue click, Felipe started the trek to the stable at the ranch. Thankfully, the remainder of the journey was uneventful, other than Blaire trying to focus on staying planted in her seat and avoiding sliding to the gunky ground again.

By the time the posse arrived at the ranch, Blaire's ankle resembled a blue basketball. It hurt so bad. The ground had dried, so at least when Felipe eased her off Thunder's back, she stood without sinking into the ground like quicksand.

"Stay here, and I'll get our things loaded on the truck and take the horses to the stable." He headed toward the barn where the adventure began and passed off both animals to the same gentleman from earlier.

The man gave him a nod of his head, but Blaire couldn't hear the interchange between them. She supposed Felipe explained why both horses were caked in mud and telling the man about Armoniá's mad dash.

Felipe shook the man's hand, and the other gentleman slapped him on the back. After loading up the truck with their bags, Felipe whisked Blaire into his strong, capable arms once again.

Blaire rolled her eyes, although she secretly enjoyed being in his arms. She cringed, thinking she probably resembled a swamp monster instead of a beautiful damsel in distress. "I can make it to the truck on my own, you know."

Raising one brow, Felipe shot a pointed glance to her monstrous ankle. "Oh, I know. However, I'd like for my clinic's sole doctor to retain the ability to walk at some point in the coming days. Based on the size of that ankle, my chances of that happening improve if I carry you."

She lifted her eyes to his, and her heart melted. Despite knowing him a short time, she felt comfortable with him, and it seemed she'd known him longer. But what would happen when it was time for her to leave? If she wanted a shot at getting her fellowship spot back, she needed to focus on her job-- taking care of people. That's it. Nothing more.

Blaire's head bobbed up and down with each sturdy step of Felipe's black boots. She gave him a cautious smile, afraid of not only encouraging him but also herself. "Um...sorry about everything." She gestured to her foot. "I guess I made a real mess of things. I'm sorry you have to carry me."

Felipe sent her a half-grin that, if she'd been standing, would've dropped her to the floor. "It's not a problem, really. How could you have known our trusty trail horse would've bolted like that. I'm glad you're not hurt worse than this." He walked a few more steps in silence and arrived at the beat-up truck.

He opened the door and lifted her inside, setting her down with care. He shut the door, walked around to the truck's driver side, and whistled for Pedro.

The old mutt lumbered along, his eyes droopy with sun and sleep. He climbed aboard his ride and plopped his head down, nestled between Blaire and the driver side seat. Within seconds his eyes shut, and he drifted off to sleep again.

Climbing in the truck, Felipe pulled the bandana out of his pocket and wiped his brow clean of perspiration. He shoved it back in and dug his keys out. Placing it in the ignition, Felipe paused, his hand still on the key. Instead of beginning the final leg of the trip home, he froze, as if thinking.

After a few seconds passed, he turned his head to Blaire and met her gaze, an intense look in his eyes. "Hey…I wanted to ask if you'd like to have dinner with me tomorrow night. Nothing too fancy or anything. I could cook, and we could take it to a special place I know and have a picnic." He raised his eyebrows and waited for her response.

Wow. She hadn't seen that coming. I mean, sure he was handsome—no denying that fact. And chivalrous, too, evidenced by his gallant rescue today during her derby experience. But…she had to go home soon. Back to her real life where fellowship, her friends, and the city awaited. And even her critical parents. She couldn't dodge them forever. *Still…it was only dinner. One dinner.*

Didn't Mabel and Tiffany encourage her to try something new…take some risks? Not be afraid to be so perfect and planned all the time? Maybe this was her chance. Before she knew what had happened, she'd opened her mouth and uttered a simple, "Yes."

She clamped her mouth shut, and heat poured into her neck and cheeks, causing them to burn. Blaire hoped he didn't notice. She was sure her face must resemble a tomato by now.

He rewarded her with a beaming grin. "Great. That's great." He turned the key in the ignition, bringing the car to life.

The engine roared, then settled into a gentle hum as it rolled down the road, away from the ranch, the horse-and-mud incident, and the elderly woman and her grandson. But not away from her thoughts of Felipe's secure embrace, his caring smile, or their upcoming dinner date. No…she had a lot to think about. *God, please tell me what all this means, what the future holds for us. Sending* a silent prayer up, Blaire waited for Him to speak to her heart.

Chapter 22

"A Watched Pot Never Boils"

Felipe stood over the black glass stovetop in the clinic's cramped kitchen, alternating between stirring polenta and keeping the creamy, white sauce on the back of the stove from burning. He gave both pots a whisk and then wiped the sweat beading on his forehead with the back of his hand. It was a hot one today. Ninety degrees.

He glanced at the old clock on the wall and noted the time. 5:30 p.m. He needed to hurry if he wanted to have the meal ready and packed in time. Tonight, he planned to take Blaire to his favorite spot in Guatemala.

Felipe told Blaire to meet him in the kitchen around 5:45 p.m. Thankfully, he'd already dressed for the evening. If he didn't soak through his clothes between the heat from the stove and the Guatemalan humidity.

After another fifteen minutes of stirring and worrying over how the evening would go, he'd packed away his mother's famous dish--the one she'd made for him as a child. It brought him comfort to experience the smells that once graced his family kitchen; cumin, chili, garlic, and peppers.

He imagined his mother with her long, black hair and elegant frame flitting about their kitchen with her floral apron tied snugly at her waist.

Lost in his thoughts, he didn't hear Juanita enter the room.

"Ahem. I said, 'It looks like you've got a big date tonight.'" She placed a hand on her plump hip and sent him a mischievous grin.

Shaking his head, Felipe tucked the last plastic container into a tattered canvas bag. "You're going to give me a hard time about this, aren't you? And read way too much into it."

Juanita's eyes widened. "Why, whatever do you mean?" She chuckled and gave Felipe a squeeze. "Have a good time. I'll see you tomorrow."

As she walked away, Felipe uttered, "Thanks." He hated it when she teased him, which was often. Since losing his mother, Juanita had stepped into a maternal role in his life, complete with plenty of elbow-ribbing and knowing looks.

Finished with his cooking and picnic planning, he walked to the sink and gave his hands a quick wash. Footsteps approached, but he continued drying his hands, not turning around. "Juanita, don't you think you gave me a hard enough time for one night? It's only a dinner date. Just two people talking and sharing a meal."

"Oh, so it's a date, is it?" Blaire's soft voice broke through his imaginary discussion with Juanita.

He dropped the black and white gingham towel he'd been drying his hands with onto the counter and turned around. Felipe's neck burned. He prayed his face didn't match the color of his crimson shirt. *What if she didn't feel the same as him?* "Hey. I thought you were Juanita." He decided to ignore her question and barrel ahead, "Are you ready to go?"

She wore a blush dress that nipped in at her waist, accentuating her slender frame. Instead of her typical high-heeled shoes, she'd replaced them with black flats and an ace bandage to the left ankle. "Yeah, I'm ready for this big dinner date." She smirked.

Smiling, Felipe took a few steps closer, closing the gap between them. As he drew nearer, he became aware of the inviting floral scent of her perfume. He marveled at how different she seemed to him now. When he'd first met her, all he'd seen was an uptight, obsessive city-slicker with too many bags. But now...now she stood before him...probably still obsessive, but also beautiful, kind, and giving. "Okay, let's go." He extended a hand to her.

She reached to accept it, taking one step toward him but winced and stumbled.

Felipe lunged forward and caught her in his arms before she fell. He searched her face for any sign of damage, brushing a strand of hair out of eyes. "Are you okay? How's your ankle? We don't have to go if you don't feel up to it."

She searched his eyes and gave him a smile. "No, I'm fine. Well...not fine. But I can make it. My ankle's not in as bad shape as I expected, given the fact I flew over the top of a horse yesterday. It's still a little tender, though."

He helped her into an upright position and offered her an arm. "Here lean on me. I'll help you. We don't have to go far, and if need be, I can carry you." He grabbed the bag filled with their meal with his other hand.

She clasped his hand and took a few cautious steps forward. Realizing she wasn't headed for another tumble, she lifted her head and grinned, tucking one of her curls behind an ear. "Thanks."

Felipe guided her out the kitchen's back door and down a small stone-covered path, flanked on either side by a canopy of tall, green trees. Reaching the end of the trail, it opened to a placid, sapphire lake. A myriad of pine and oak trees speckled the perimeter of the body of water. A fresh vanilla scent mixed with lemongrass carried a sweet aroma through the air on a gentle breeze.

Blaire gasped. "It's gorgeous! It looks like a painting in a museum. I've never seen anything so breathtaking in my life."

He nodded his head and let go of her hand. Retrieving a red and white square-patterned quilt from his canvas bag, Felipe spread it across the ground. He placed the food containers on top of the blanket. Then, he turned to her, spreading his hands in the presentation of the feast. "All set." Taking her hand in his, he lowered Blaire onto the blanket, trying to avoid causing more pain to her ankle.

She beamed at him. "Thank you for bringing me here. If I lived here, I'd come here every day." Blaire smoothed her dress and then tilted her head, setting her gaze upon him.

He returned her grin. "Yeah, I came here all the time when I was a kid. My dad took me fishing on the weekends, and my brothers and I swam here daily during summer break. Somehow, along the way, it became my special spot, my favorite place."

"Well, thanks for sharing it with me."

Felipe moved his eyes away from her and opened the containers one at a time. He handed her a plate. "You're welcome. You're the first person I've brought here besides my family." He hesitated before meeting her eyes again.

"I'm honored." Blaire took the plate from him, scooped some of the polenta dish onto her paper plate, and poured iced tea into a paper cup. "This looks amazing. Thank you for making it. I can't cook at all…unless you count microwaving a frozen dinner."

He chuckled, dishing out food for himself as well. "No problem."

Blaire lifted the fork to her lips but paused. "So, does your family still live nearby?"

Felipe's stomach clenched. The shackles securing his heart had opened during his time spent with Blaire, and he'd started to let her inside. Hearing the word "family" threatened to lock them back into place. He didn't know if he could trust her with his story; if he could open up to her completely.

She must have noticed his change in demeanor because she laid a gentle hand on top of his. "Hey, I didn't mean to upset you."

He stared at her hand, and something within him was released. Felipe didn't know why, but he knew he could trust Blaire. He wanted to trust her. "No, it's okay. I don't have any family left. A few years ago, a mudslide wiped out a large section of the town...including all of my family."

Blaire's hand flew to her mouth. "Oh, Felipe, I'm sorry... that's horrible...I had no idea."

He shrugged. "Not your fault. But that's why this town, or what's left of it anyway, is so important to me. When it happened...I was away at college. I came home to help with the clean-up and couldn't bring myself to leave again. I owed it to my family and the town to make it up to them...I should've been here. Maybe I could've done something."

Blaire scooted closer and draped her hand on his shoulder. Giving it a gentle squeeze, she tilted her head, forcing him to meet her gaze. "Hey. You didn't know. You couldn't have stopped it. This town is blessed to have you here, and you're doing a great job caring for the community. It's a special place." She stared out at the lake and sighed. "I can see why you stayed."

Looking overhead into the darkening sky, Felipe wondered if rain was coming. Brooding clouds hovered above, threatening to cut the evening short. He cleared his throat. "I hate to say it, but it looks like a storm's on the way. We better pack up and head inside."

As if giving his premonition a stamp of confirmation, thunder rumbled. A few small raindrops fell, pelting his arms and encouraging him to move quicker.

He shoved the remainder of the romantic dinner into the canvas bag and lifted Blaire to a standing position. Guiding her up the trail to the clinic's back door, he kept his hand under her arm so she could lean on him.

As she topped the hill, Blaire stumbled, and Felipe heard her groan.

Without speaking a word, Felipe swept her into his arms, carrying her the rest of the way. When he arrived at the kitchen door, the dim light from the outdoor sconce provided another glimpse of her sapphire eyes and slightly flushed cheeks.

He wanted to kiss her. What would it mean if he did? As far as Felipe knew, she planned to leave at the end of the month, and then he'd be alone again. Could he trust her with his heart? Searching her face for answers, a loud crack of lightning lit up the night sky, startling him.

Heavy waters poured from the sky, soaking their clothes.

"Agh," Blaire shrieked. "Hurry, let's get under there." She gestured to the awning atop the backdoor to the clinic's kitchen.

Felipe carried her to the door and sat her down, still looking into her eyes. He brushed his hand across her cheek, cupping her sweet face. "I almost forgot to ask you… there's this party… it's sort of a community event--the whole town comes. There's a buffet of amazing food, great music, dancing. That sort of thing."

She grinned. "Sounds fun. When is it?"

"Friday night…would you like to go with me?"

Blaire grabbed both of his hands and gave them a squeeze. "I'd love to go. I don't know about the buffet—you know, my thing about germs—but the rest of it seems perfect. It's a date."

He grinned and held the door open for her. "It's a date."

Chapter 23

"Love is Blind"

Blaire slid her foot into a flat sandal. The week passed in a blur since her "non-date date" with Felipe. The clinic's busy pace combined with the pleasant nervousness she experienced while in his presence made each day both exciting and anxiety riddled.

She plucked a cleansing wipe from her bag and gave each hand a swipe, realizing it was the first one she'd used that day. Hmm...perhaps Felipe was a good distraction.

A knock sounded at her bedroom door, interrupting her thoughts. Blaire walked to the door and opened it.

Felipe caught his breath at the sight of her, and his eyes widened. "You look great. Ready to go?" He extended a hand to her.

"I'm ready." She tossed her purse over her shoulder and walked with more ease out the door than she'd mustered at the end of their last date. Thankfully, her ankle had shrunk to a reasonable size, and the black and blue pigments had faded to an ill-looking green. Still—an improvement.

Glancing down at her indigo spaghetti-strapped dress, Blaire smoothed the skirt, which ended just below her knees. Her cheeks flushed at his compliment, though it pleased her. She caught his eye and rewarded him with a smile. "Thanks. You, too. I mean, you look great, too." She clasped her hand in his and followed him downstairs and into the balmy evening air.

As they exited the building, he passed her a small rock. "Here." She raised her forehead. "What's this for?"

Sending her a half-grin, he responded, calm and collected, "For the wild dogs."

Horrified, Blaire clutched her chest. "There are wild dogs? And you plan to...what? Throw a rock at them?" Even though dogs weren't her favorite animal, she'd grown fonder of the clinic canine and could never bring herself to hurt another creature."

Shaking his head, Felipe chuckled. "No, no. We're not going to throw it at the dog. The thing is there are a lot of rogue dogs and even rattlesnakes here, so if something unexpected crosses our path, we can toss these near it to scare it away." He put a hand in the air. "I promise I won't hurt anything or anyone. Unless it's about to attack you."

She let out the breath she'd been holding. "Okay, well, good. That's good to hear. But...snakes?"

He laughed again and strolled with Blaire, guiding her through the small town to the site of the party.

He stopped in front of a wrought-iron archway, flanked by blue vine sage, and gestured for her to go ahead of him. "Here we are."

Blaire walked through the entryway and noted the pleasant aroma of jasmine and vanilla. Beyond the front gate, Blaire's eyes landed on a white and teal wood-planked house with a thatched roof. She peered over her shoulder, giving her attention to Felipe. "Whose house is this?"

Felipe joined her and grinned. "It's Juanita's. Pretty great, huh?"

Scanning the estate before her, she had to agree. Although the house was small, the land surrounding it was not. She glanced at Felipe again. "Does she own all of this?"

He nodded. "Sure does. Juanita lost all of her family in the mudslide, too. She was visiting friends in Guatemala City when it hit. Her house was one of the few spared in the slide, but her family was working on a farm that got hit. Since then, she's dedicated herself to the clinic and rebuilding the community...and her garden."

How does someone recover from such a loss? Blaire had only lost her sister, but still, that was enough. It had changed the course of the rest of her life. She couldn't imagine losing her entire family, difficult though they were. "At least you two have each other."

A solemn look washed over Felipe's face. "Yeah. She's been the person I could count on for years...I trust her." As quickly as the somber moment arrived, it left, and he replaced the firm line of his lips with a hopeful smile. "Well, enough of that talk for the evening. Come on."

Blaire shifted her gaze away from his and stood in awe of the festivities before her. Felipe hadn't lied when he'd said the entire town came to these things. Soft, votive lights inside glass mason jars hung with thin wire from lower branches of sweeping, lush trees. Varying sized tables swathed in brightly colored tablecloths provided sitting areas for people to eat and converse. Chatter and laughter filled the air along with the sounds of merengue music.

A long table held the buffet. It overflowed with a bounty of empanadas, tortillas, plantains, and a myriad of other culinary delights. The waft of food and friends carried a sweet, inviting fragrance. With each passing day, she reminded herself she would have to leave soon. It was getting harder and harder to remember this fact. She'd grown attached to the community and its people. As this thought drifted through Blaire's mind, Juanita sauntered over, her hips swaying to the salsa music with each step.

Juanita reached in and gathered Blaire into a fierce embrace, not bothering with formalities. "Hola, mi amiga. How are you doing on this beautiful evening God made for us?"

Blaire cast a smile at Juanita and gave her a gentle squeeze. "I'm good, Juanita, thanks for asking."

Planting her hands on her hips, Juanita grinned proudly. "Pretty amazing, isn't it? This town sure knows how to throw a party! We may not have a lot, but what we do have, we share with one another." She glanced between Blaire and Felipe, and her mouth formed a knowing grin. "So, I see that Sr. Martinez decided to escort you this evening. Very good."

She addressed Felipe. "Well, don't just stand there, Felipe, get some food in this girl's belly and get her feet moving on the dance floor. You're both too young to stand here like rooted trees—you need to enjoy life!"

Felipe raised both hands in the air in concession. "Okay, okay. You got it, Juanita. I'm on it." He turned to Blaire and offered his hand. "Come on...you haven't lived until you've tried Juanita's empanadas--life-changing." He looked to Juanita for confirmation.

Her grin widened, and she acted humble, but Blaire could tell she was pleased. Juanita waved his flattery away. "Oh, you exaggerate." She lowered her voice to a conspiratorial whisper and leaned in close to Blaire's ear, "But you really must try one. They're my mother's secret recipe, and I won't say they are life-changing, but they do have a history of bringing together couples and blessing them with love." She winked toward Felipe.

Warmth filled Blaire's chest and rose upward to her neck and cheeks. She tucked her head down, embarrassed. Blaire peeked at Felipe to see if he'd heard Juanita's teasing comment, but he seemed distracted by the prospect of eating good food.

She flicked her eyes back to Juanita to tell her she wouldn't miss the empanadas, but Juanita had started chatting with another couple nearby.

Felipe squeezed Blaire's hand to get her attention and led her to the buffet. He loaded his plate full of food and wore an expression of glee, like a child on Christmas morning. He grabbed several items with his bare hands and stacked a series of foods on sticks on his plate like a game.

Blaire took a more conservative approach. Sure, she wanted to live life with joy, relax, take things as they came…but she couldn't release all of her inhibitions. Eating food off a buffet proved a considerable challenge for Blaire. Baby steps. She wasn't about to leap ahead to picking things up with her bare fingers like Felipe.

She discreetly slid a plastic fork out of her bag and tore the plastic wrapper off of it. After tucking the trash in her purse, she used her fresh, germ-free utensil to pick the most sensible items off the table and place them on her plate.

Compared to Felipe's teetering tower of food, Blaire's looked sparse. She'd concluded cooked plantains were her safest bet. After all, they had their own built-in wrapper by way of a peel. So, that had to help decrease the potential germ-load.

After selecting her food, Blaire followed Felipe and sat down at a small two-top table covered in handmade white linen with a tea-light candle in the center.

Felipe placed his plate down and walked around to pull out Blaire's chair for her.

Blaire sat down, tucking her skirt underneath her. She lifted her eyes to him and sent him a smile. "Thanks." He placed his hand on her upper back as she took her place and the touch of his hand sent a shiver tingling down her spine.

He glanced at her plate as he took his seat and raised his eyebrows. "Is that all you're going to eat?"

She stared at her meager plate of plantains and a pile of cooked rice and felt a flush creeping into her cheeks again. "Well…yes. I'm not that hungry…and besides…I have a hard time with germs. Remember?"

His eyes softened and nodded, seeming to understand her plight. "Let's say grace." He held his hand out palm up, ready to receive her hand.

She accepted it, bowed her head, and closed her eyes.

"Father God, we thank you for this food prepared by blessed, clean hands, for a night of fun, and for friends filled with acceptance and love. Thank you for making old things new and giving us beauty for ashes. Amen." Felipe raised his head and let his hand linger on hers.

His prayer touched her heart, making her feel welcome and understood.

Her shoulders relaxed, and she marveled at how at ease, he made her feel. Her stomach growled, and she dug in, eating quickly, realizing she'd skipped lunch.

They ate in silence for several minutes, and once they'd finished, Felipe leaned back in his chair and flashed her a smile. "Would you do me the honor of dancing with me?"

Blaire looked toward other couples dancing and imagined Felipe holding her in his arms. Her palms began to sweat. "Oh, I don't know… I'm a terrible dancer. Plus, I happen to have firsthand knowledge of the damage you can inflict on people's toes. My pinkie toe may not recover after another insult."

He gave her a deadpan stare, then broke into a grin. "Funny. Hilarious. Now, come on. I promise not to damage any more of your toes."

She rose, following him to the makeshift dance floor in the center of the lawn. Overhead the twinkle lights strung in layers, and the votives hanging from branches cast a soft, romantic glow.

Felipe turned to face her, placing one hand in hers and the other behind her back. He swayed back and forth in time to the slow music, holding her close.

Resting her head on Felipe's firm shoulder, she melted in his arms. "Thanks. For everything," she murmured.

"What do you mean? You're the one who saved my life in New York."

She lifted her head and met his gaze. "I mean, thanks for all of it. For welcoming me, for saving me on the horse, for sharing your community with me. For the first time in my life, I feel...accepted. Like I might be enough. That probably sounds silly...but thanks."

He brushed a strand of her hair off her forehead and grew serious. "No problem. And you are enough. You're more than enough. God says so, and so do I." He leaned in closer and whispered, "Will you come with me?" his lips grazing her ear.

Blaire's ear tingled, and her heart pounded. She gave a small nod. "Sure."

~

Felipe couldn't take his eyes off Blaire all evening. She was a beautiful woman, there was no denying that fact. But tonight, she stunned him. She'd ripped open his heart and torn down his walls.

He guided her through Juanita's backyard to a trail connected to the same lake he'd taken Blaire on their first date. The lake looked more pristine tonight, if possible. The evening sun dipped below the skyline casting rays of orange, red, and purple across the sky and reflected off the surface of the lake, making it all the more brilliant.

Once they arrived at the edge of the lake, he sat down and patted the ground next to him.

Blaire settled on the grass beside him and smiled. "It's so lovely tonight."

"Yes, it's lovely...and so are you." He turned his head, staring into Blaire's eyes.

"I can't believe I've only been here for a few weeks. It's started to feel like...home. The people...well...they make it hard to think about leaving."

The sun fell beyond the horizon, cloaking everything in twilight. He should have felt safer, more concealed, but instead, Felipe had never felt more exposed and vulnerable in his life. "I guess we should head back. It's getting late."

"You're probably right." She made no sign of movement.

He leaned in closer, searching her face for answers. *How much longer would she stay? Would she leave at the end of her month? Would he see her again?* He placed a hand gently on her chin and tilted her mouth closer to his. Felipe pressed his lips against hers softly at first, then with more urgency, and the remainder of those shackles around his heart fell away.

Blaire answered his questions with tenderness, melting further into his embrace. With a final kiss, she lifted her head, smiling up at him through dark eyelashes.

As Felipe stood riveted, he could not recall the last time he'd been this happy--he prayed it would last. He prayed she might stay because if he searched his own heart, he'd discover a yearning to call Dr. Blaire Cunningham his wife someday.

~

A few days later, Blaire dressed for clinic in scrub pants and a simple white t-shirt and pulled her hair back in a low ponytail. She peered at her reflection in a compact mirror she'd retrieved from her purse. *Not bad.* Other than the slightly dark circles underneath her eyes.

She'd hardly slept last night, her thoughts drifting to the heart-pounding kiss she'd shared with Felipe. What did it mean? And what would happen in a few weeks when she had to leave?

Staring at her lips in the reflection, Blaire pressed her fingertips to them and closed her eyes. It was an epic kiss. If she wasn't careful, she'd fall in love with Felipe, and then what would she do? She couldn't stay here if she wanted a chance to finish her fellowship. Plus, the gala for Megan loomed on the horizon. It wasn't that Blaire didn't want to celebrate her sister's memory. Quite the opposite. She recalled a conversation she'd had with her sister the night before Megan left for college.

"Hey, little sis, why the sad face?" Megan's blue eyes, crinkled, concern clouding their usual brightness. Her blond hair cast a golden halo around her head and embodied the goodness that Blaire's sister embodied.

A tear trailed down Blaire's cheek, soon to be followed by many more. She rubbed them away with her fingertips, determined to push them, and her feelings back down from where they came. Cunningham's didn't show emotion; they were stoic. "Oh, Megan...I feel like I'll never see you again."

Megan joined Blaire on the bed.

Sitting in her big sister's room, Blaire scanned the comforter and trimmings boasting an upper-crust French vibe designed by their mother. The walls betrayed the image with a myriad of posters Megan had hung of famous rock bands. "I still can't believe mother let you keep those on the walls...it just goes to show you're the golden child—you can do no wrong."

Megan shook her head and sent her little sister a half-smile. She stroked Blaire's hair. "Don't cry, little sis. You'll see me. Sooner than you think. I'll be home for Thanksgiving, a month at Christmas, and you can join me for a weekend or two if mom and dad let you. Plus, there's the church mission trip over spring break...maybe mom will let you come with me."

Blaire rolled her eyes. "Haha. Yeah, right. You, they let run around the country, becoming anything you want. You do everything well; school, cheerleading, student government. And you make it look easy. Not to mention you're gorgeous, and mother loves showing you off to her society friends. You fit inside their box. And even when you don't, they're so mesmerized by you, they just redraw the box. Meanwhile, I'm way over here outside the box."

Megan patted her sister's shoulder. "Hey, look at me."

Blaire lifted her head slowly, finally meeting Megan's eyes. More tears burst forth. How would she manage without Megan? Megan was her buffer at home. She kept things civil between Blaire and her parents. She shuddered to think what life would look like around the Cunningham camp once Megan-less.

"Listen to me. You're wonderful. Exactly how God made you. You are perfect in his eyes. That's all that matters. You don't have to worry about me leaving, because I'm a phone call away and we will see each other lots. I promise. And mom and dad love you. I know they have a funny way of showing it and sometimes their expectations are…high—"

Blaire snorted. "Ya think?"

Megan chuckled, then continued, "But you don't have to try to meet them. The expectations, I mean. Just be you, Blaire, because that's a pretty incredible person to be. I love you lots, little sis."

"I love you more." Blaire squeezed her sister with all the might in her eighth-grader arms. "You're going to change the world. You'll probably work for the Volunteer Corps or become a lawyer for abused children."

Megan smiled. "Or a missionary…maybe a doctor?"

Blaire snapped back to reality. She hadn't thought about that conversation in years. It had been the last time Blaire had spoken with Megan in person. A month into Megan's first year at university, she'd contracted meningitis, and the rest was…well, history.

Choking down the grief that tried to resurrect itself, Blaire stumbled downstairs to join Felipe and Juanita for coffee before seeing the first patient of the day.

She entered the kitchen, resting her hand on the archway. She prepared herself for an awkward interchange with Felipe, but he wasn't there.

Juanita stood in front of the coffee pot, pouring the delicious hot liquid into a ceramic mug. She lifted her head and looked at Blaire. "Want a cup?"

Blaire sent her a thankful smile and nodded. "That'd be great. I didn't sleep well last night."

Juanita arched a brow. "No? Didn't you have a good time at the party this weekend?"

"Oh, it wasn't that. The party was great. Your food was amazing, and I enjoyed dancing…no, I had a wonderful time."

Her colleague and new-found confidant's brow rose higher. "How wonderful of a time?" She sent a sideways glance to Blaire.

Walking closer to Juanita, Blaire gave a playful swat at her friend's arm. "Juanita! I can't believe you. Do you know something?"

Now it was Juanita's turn to smirk. She planted one hand on her hip and handed a full mug of coffee to Blaire with the other one. "Just murmurings around town that you and Felipe slipped away at the party. That combined with the red flush in your cheeks. I'm older, but I'm not dead. I pick up on these things. You like him, don't you?"

Embarrassed, Blaire tucked her head down and took a draw from her coffee. It warmed her soul, and though she had no intention of spilling her emotions to Juanita, the words tumbled from her mouth, "I do like him...a lot."

Juanita clapped her hands together. "That's wonderful!"

"But does it matter? I don't have much time here. If I don't go home, I'll miss the gala in honor of my sister and blow any chance of rejoining my fellowship. I'm still waiting on the final word from my director to see if he'll give me a second chance."

"And if he didn't? If he didn't give you a second chance...would that be so bad? Would it be so terrible to stay here with us? You're fitting in, and the community seems to love you. I think someone else may love you, too. He's just bull-headed and stubborn about letting people in."

Blaire stared at her wise friend for a second and then shrugged. "Maybe. Maybe he feels the same way...but my life is in New York. My parents, as difficult as they may be, are in New York. My career, my responsibilities, my expectations...are in New York."

Juanita gave a small nod. "Okay. I hear you. But can I give you a piece of advice?"

Tilting her head, Blaire smiled. "Sure, what is it?"

"Don't be bull-headed and stubborn, too. And don't live your life by someone else's expectations. Your life doesn't have to look perfect or be perfect. You don't have to be perfect. God loves you. And other people want to love you...be open to letting them. Okay?"

Blaire caught her breath, thinking back to her sister's same words years ago. She paused before answering, "Okay," and gave a shuddering breath.

Blaire swallowed the remainder of her coffee and rinsed out the cup, placing it beside the sink upside down to dry. She headed to one of the exam rooms to prepare for what promised to be a long, busy day. As she exited the kitchen, she bumped into Felipe, and he narrowly missed stepping on her foot again.

"Hey, watch it. I don't think my toe can survive a second attack by you." She smiled. Her face burned standing so near him as she felt his warm breath near her cheek.

He stared into her eyes and grinned. "Hey," he placed his hands up, "not my fault this time. You looked like you were on a mission."

"I am on a mission. I'm heading to the exam room to make sure it's stocked for the day." She glanced at her watch, checking the time. *7:45 a.m.* "Cutting it close, aren't you?" The corner of her lips formed a teasing smile.

"Thanks for the reminder. Sorry, I woke up late, and I spent some time with God before heading down. I'll be there in a few minutes. I'm going to grab a quick cup of coffee. Okay?"

"Okay." She slid past him, trying to put aside thoughts of how he'd made her pulse race when he kissed her.

He placed a gentle hand on her arm, stopping her retreat.

His caress sent a jolt of electricity through her. She turned toward him and murmured, "Yeah?"

He stepped closer, and his eyes grew serious. "About the other night…"

Blaire dropped her head. She knew she'd made it all up in her mind. Fabricated things. Sure, they'd shared a kiss, but maybe that's all it was to him; a kiss. "Yeah, it was…"

Felipe placed both hands on her face and looked into her eyes. "It was incredible. You are incredible. Thanks for going with me to the party."

Was he going to kiss her again? Here, in the clinic?

For a moment, she thought he would, but then he dropped his

hands, tossed her an easy grin, and said, "I'll see you back there." He walked away to the kitchen, whistling as he left.

Her knees now mush, Blaire gathered herself and spun around, determined to focus on the work of the day. But she couldn't erase the memory of the kiss, the promise of the next one, and the hope of a future she knew couldn't come for her and Mr. Felipe Martinez.

Chapter 24

"And They Lived Happily Ever After?"

To: Felipe Martinez
From: The Mayor of Santiago del Alma
Subject: Clinic closure

Mr. Martinez,

With a heavy heart, I inform you that the City Council and I voted to close La Clinica, effective August 9, 2019 at midnight, if you cannot secure a permanent physician to oversee the facility by then. The city needs the space for other projects, and the Council agreed with my concerns about the liability of having the clinic open without physician supervision.

Thank you again for your time and dedication to La Clinica and the Santiago del Alma community.

Respectfully,

Mayor of Santiago del Alma

Felipe sat at his desk in his cramped office, staring at the white sheet before him. He'd spent the majority of his week attempting to focus on patient care and clinic schedules. Felipe found it challenging, given the distraction of working aside Blaire.

He'd thought she was beautiful the first time he met her on the sidewalk in New York. Felipe remembered staring into her eyes after he had landed on her and thinking they looked like pools of sapphire. Now, though, he'd had time to discover the loveliness of her spirit and the kindness in her heart. Sure, she had a thing for excessive usage of hand sanitizers, but what once he found irritating became an endearing quirk.

The letter before him pulled his thoughts from Blaire and her blue eyes and back to the reality of the timeline he faced. Two weeks. That's it. Two weeks was all he had—two weeks to save the clinic.

Felipe pounded his fist on the desk. He couldn't give up. Even though it looked grim. Still…there was a morsel of hope Blaire would stay past the end of the month…maybe even forever. Oh, who was he kidding? Mostly, himself. Shaking his head, he glared at the vile letter. A knock on the door startled him, and he straightened his posture.

"Sorry, I didn't mean to scare you." Blaire stood at the doorway, one hand on the doorframe for support. She tilted her head to the side and smiled.

A wide grin spread across his face, and his shoulders relaxed. He waved for her to join him in the cramped space. "You didn't scare me…well, you did, but it's okay." He nodded toward the laptop sitting on his desk. "I was going over some paperwork, emails, that sort of thing. What can I do for you? Not that I'm not happy to see you. Because I am," he flirted, sending her an encouraging smile.

Blaire stepped in and stood in front of the desk. She shifted her weight. "Uh, I wanted to see if I could borrow your computer when you're finished here? I need to check my email. I tried to call my best friends back home earlier today, but I couldn't get a signal with my cellphone. I'm sure they're worried about me or at least interested in how comical it's been having germaphobic Blaire in the great outdoors."

Felipe rose from his chair and covered the letter on his desk with a blank piece of writing paper. He ran a hand through his hair and gestured for her to take his seat. "Sure, no problem. I need to check on some things in the clinic anyways. The laptop is open and turned on, so you just need to log on to your email. Pretty easy."

Blaire walked to the seat and sank down. She looked up at Felipe and sent him a gentle smile that lit up her eyes. "Thanks."

Standing near Blaire caused his pulse to race. He stared into her eyes filled with kindness, and his heart softened further. Placing a hand on her shoulder, he couldn't deny she stirred his heart. "You look beautiful today. Thank you for your help at the clinic. We're fortunate to have you. And you're doing a great job."

Blaire blushed, her cheeks deepening to a crimson shade. She whispered a soft, "Thanks."

Felipe bent down and brought his face within inches of hers. He brushed his lips against hers, and his heart beat faster. He pulled away and paused. "You're welcome," he breathed before rising and leaving the office.

Two weeks. Two weeks for God to work a miracle and convince Blaire to stay. He uttered a quick prayer and tried to put the letter along with the looming deadline out of his mind.

~

Blaire sat in the wooden chair in Felipe's office and ran both hands over the curved, worn armrests. She pulled the laptop toward her and raised her hands, ready to click open the browser and pull up her email.

As her finger hovered above the mouse, the edge of a paper on the desk caught her attention. She couldn't read all of it because a plain sheet of paper covered it, but the subject line poked out the side. It read "Clinic closure."

Lifting her head, Blaire glanced at the empty doorway, searching to see if anyone was around. The hallway remained empty, and she peered at the paper once more. She shouldn't snoop through Felipe's things--it wasn't her business. But...the words clinic closure lingered in her mind. Hey, if the clinic closes and she could have done something to help...funding...or whatever...well, she considered it a moral obligation to take a peek at the form—just a peak.

Blaire scooted her hand to the plain white paper. She inched it off the hidden sheet below. *Oh, wow.* It wasn't much a surprise...not really. She knew Felipe had mentioned he'd had problems keeping staff in the clinic. But when he'd discussed the clinic's fate before, she'd not been as invested.

Now...her heart lay on the line. And her career. A thought tickled her brain. She could stay here in Guatemala and work at the clinic...with Felipe...she didn't have to go home. But if she didn't return home, she'd have no chance of completing her Infectious Disease Fellowship. No chance at all. *What would Megan say? What would Megan do?*

Blaire turned her attention to the laptop and opened her email account in the browser. Hoping to get word to her two best friends and gain their insight to her evolving...situation, Blaire banged on the keys, crafting an email to Mabel and Tiffany.

Hey guys,

Things are going better than expected here. I love working in the clinic, and every day is different and surprising. The cases can be challenging, but the people are wonderful. Very welcoming. I sent my email to Dr. Sedgewick about my experience to prove I've handled new challenges. I can't believe I'm saying this, but part of me wants to stay here. Plus, there's Felipe--he kissed me. More than once. I don't know what it means...maybe nothing...but it doesn't feel like nothing. Pray for me, girls.

All my love,
Blaire

Blaire hit the send button, and the compose window on her email account closed. Bold, blue letters called her attention on the screen. In the inbox, an item read:

From: Dr. Michael Sedgewick, To: Dr. Blaire Cunningham, Subject: Fellowship.

Her finger hovered over the link, ready to open the message. She closed her eyes and pulled in a deep breath. The only way to know what it said was to open it. She double-clicked on the foreboding letters and opened both eyes.

To: Dr. Blaire Cunningham
    From: Dr. Michael Sedgewick, Program Director at New York Memorial School of Medicine, Department of Infectious Disease
Subject: Fellowship
Dr. Cunningham,
    As per my last communication, I'm agreeable to considering your re-admittance to the Infectious Disease Fellowship Program if you can show an ability to work in unpredictable and new situations. I reviewed the summarization of your work abroad and found it

encouraging. If you are still interested in the Infectious Disease Fellowship Post-Graduate Year Two position, please submit a letter of intent to me by the end of the week. Barring anything unforeseen, I might consider your return to the program on a probationary basis. If the first six months went smoothly, then I would remove the probationary status.
Sincerely,
Dr. Michael Sedgewick

Blaire stared at the black and white words on the screen and swallowed hard--a second chance. That's what it said. She had a second chance to prove herself, to show she could do it and was worthy, good enough.

But if she grabbed this opportunity, she'd have to leave Guatemala and Felipe behind...forever. She exhaled the breath she'd been holding. Everything she'd fought for since Megan passed lay before her. Blaire closed her eyes. She wasn't prone to praying outside of scripted suppertime blessings, goodnight whispers, or during a near-death horseback ride, but something tugged at her heart.

Her structured, religious parents had taken her to church as a child but raised her to be seen, not heard...by everyone. That included God. God seemed distant from Blaire most of her life.

The tugging drew her closer to something...something bigger than herself. "Hey...God...uh, it's me, Blaire," she whispered. "I don't know if I'm doing this right...but, uh, I'm kind of dealing with a hard decision. I want to honor Megan's memory and prove to everyone...including my parents, I can do it...I can finish fellowship. I can make a difference my own way, not theirs. I know my mother doesn't get it...and I guess it might not even change her perception of me...but it feels like I have to try. But...I don't want to leave. I don't want to leave all these people, this clinic, or Felipe. Maybe this is how it's supposed to be...maybe it's the sacrifice I have to make. I don't deserve all this love…all this happiness. Not after Megan lost her life. I don't know…I don't know what I'm asking for here. I guess some guidance or a miraculous solution…uh, thanks."

As she raised her head, Blaire heard Juanita calling her name.

"Dr. Cunningham. Dr. Cunningham? Where are you hiding?"

Blaire heard footsteps approaching the office door. She glanced at the open laptop and slammed it shut, forgetting to close her email browser. "In here, Juanita. I checked my email. I'm coming." She rose from the chair and stretched her arms overhead, leaning side to side, working the kinks out of her back. Blaire walked to the doorway as Juanita approached.

"Dr. Cunningham."

"Blaire, please…please call me Blaire."

Juanita grinned, and her sun-tanned skin crinkled around her eyes. She gave a small nod. "Okay. Blaire, then. It's getting late, and I'm about to head home, but I wanted to ask you for a favor."

Blaire lifted her forehead. "Sure, how can I help?"

Searching to see if anyone else was around, the nurse stalled, "Well…" She met Blaire's gaze again and paused.

"Really, it's fine. Whatever it is, if I can do it, then I'm happy to help."

Juanita dipped her head. "Okay. The thing is… I've had high blood pressure for years, and I take medication for it, no problem. Usually, I feel fine, and I feel silly for mentioning it…but…" she trailed off, dropping her eyes to the ground.

Frowning, Blaire couldn't hide her concern. "But what, Juanita?

Rubbing her left arm, Juanita lifted her head. "But today during clinic, my left arm ached…something I've never felt before. And my face felt warm…not hot like a fever…just warm."

Blaire paused, holding her hand above Juanita's shoulder, debating what to do next. She laid it on the nurse's shoulder and asked, "Why don't you follow me to an exam room and let's take a look. At least take your vitals and give your heart and lungs a listen."

After a few seconds of debating, Juanita caved, "Okay, but I've got to get home and have supper with my husband. He'll be worried about me if I take much longer. He'll think I got lost or something."

Relief coursed through Blaire's veins, and she gestured with her hand for Juanita to lead the way down the hallway to an empty exam room. Blaire flicked on the light switch, and the dim light cast a foreboding, yellow glow around the space.

Pointing to the exam table, Blaire guided her new friend, advisor, and patient to take a seat. She cleaned her hands and started her exam. "Okay, let's see what we've got." Blaire retrieved a blood pressure cuff from a drawer and wrapped the device around Juanita's arm, securing the Velcro. Then, she removed her stethoscope from her neck and tucked the bell inside the cuff. A few pumps tightened the cuff, and Blaire released the valve, watching the needle tick around the dial as she listened. *Normal. Huh.*

Removing the device, Blaire announced, "125/80. So, your blood pressure is normal." She placed her fingertips on Juanita's wrist and checked her pulse. After listening to the lungs and heart, Blaire relaxed further. "So far, Juanita, everything looks good."

The visible tension in Juanita's stiff posture eased. "That's a relief. I told you… I'm probably just being a silly old woman…a worrywart."

Blaire placed a hand on top of Juanita's. "You're not silly, and you're not old. And the worrywart part…well, that's my domain." She chuckled.

Juanita shook her head. "You shouldn't worry. You're too young and have too much life ahead of you…you need to enjoy it. Trust God and let go. Isn't that what the Good Book says? Hmm?"

Trust God and let go. "Hey, can I ask you something?"

"After all you've done for this clinic and me? Sure."

"If I leave at the end of the month and go home…is there anyone else Felipe can get to come in here…I mean, doctor wise?"

Juanita's face sagged. "No, he's tried. And tried and tried. I know he's a determined young man, so I doubt he'll give up until the last second. But…I don't see a logical way for the clinic to stay open. We've been told several times if we don't have a physician on staff regularly, then they will close us. It's a shame."

"But all these people…they need care. Who will take care of them?" Tears threatened to spill onto Blaire's cheeks.

Juanita's eyes clouded. "I don't know, dear. I don't know. But that's not for you to fret over. You have your life to return to…and a fellowship to rejoin. Unless…"

Placing the stethoscope around her neck, Blaire widened her eyes. "Unless what?"

Juanita pressed on, "Unless there's someone, in particular, you care for…love even, and wanted to stay."

Blaire's busied herself with returning the blood pressure cuff to its rightful home. "Well…"

"Yes, dear?"

Fiddling with her stethoscope, Blaire gathered her thoughts. She could stay. *Why not?* Oh, because she promised, no vowed, to Megan, she would make a difference. She needed to finish her fellowship. Blaire pledged to herself to make her parent's proud. If she stayed… she'd be setting all those promises aside. "Uh…well… I'd like to stay. Really, I would. I'd like to pause time and be with Felipe. I think I love him. But is love enough? Am I enough? If I don't go back to finish what I started… aren't I giving up?" Blaire turned around and slowly raised her eyes to meet Juanita's.

Juanita cleared her throat and waved her younger friend over. "Come here. Come closer."

Blaire obliged and stood silently in front of Juanita.

Juanita placed both hands on Blaire's shoulders and gave her a squeeze. "Listen…none of us are enough…not really, not on our own. But God tells us that His grace is enough, His power is enough…and His love is enough. We are made perfect in our weakness. So, honey, you don't have to be enough. You don't have to be anything other than a child of God. In my opinion, Felipe loves you, too. For what it's worth. And love is a gift."

Staring at her friend for a beat longer, Blaire begged the tears pooling in her eyes to abate. As one teetered over the brink, she wiped it away and let out a shuddering breath. "Thanks, Juanita." She glanced at the ground and whispered, "Thank you."

After a final squeeze, Juanita said, "You're welcome, dear. Now I've got to get home, or my gift known as my husband is going to starve to death."

Blaire heard the footsteps of her friend and advisor walking away, and by the time she lifted her head, Juanita was gone.

Chapter 25

"Mind Your Own Business"

Felipe walked down the hallway, noting how quiet the clinic had become. Each footstep echoed in his ear. He wondered if Blaire was still in the office. The thought of seeing her again caused him to smile.

As he approached the office, he saw the door stood open. With a grin in place, he leaned his head through the doorway. "Blaire, I wanted to know—"

His eyes fell upon the empty chair behind his untidy desk. Disappointed, his smile faded, and he glanced at his watch, debating whether to do paperwork or call it a night. *7:00 p.m. Not so late.*

He strode to the chair and settled into it. After lifting the laptop lid, his gaze landed on the open email account in front of him. Within a few seconds, he realized the account didn't belong to him; it belonged to Blaire. He shouldn't read it--it wasn't his business, but he couldn't help noting the sender and subject line.

From: Dr. Michael Sedgewick, Subject: Fellowship.

Felipe chided himself for even considering violating Blaire's trust by reading the email. He closed his eyes, willing himself to make the right decision, but instead, he opened his eyes and double-clicked the link.

After a minute of scanning the message from Blaire's former boss, Felipe's pulse pounded, and his throat tightened. *She would leave.* He'd known it was the most likely scenario--that her time here was temporary, but this provided confirmation. And then he'd be alone again. He pounded his fist on the desk, causing the table to shake.

After closing the laptop, Felipe rushed out of the office, flicking the light off and slamming the door behind him. He placed both hands against the closed door, hanging his head.

Leaning in, he took slow, steady breaths. *Pull it together.* After a couple of long breaths, Felipe stood upright and pushed away from the door. No...he couldn't let her leave. He'd lost everyone else he cared about years ago...he could not lose Blaire. With renewed purpose and hope in his heart, Felipe walked down the hallway, up the stairwell, and stopped in front of Blaire's door.

He raised his hand to knock but realized the door was open a sliver. As he placed his hand on it, he heard Blaire's voice speaking to someone else and paused. *Walk away.* But his curiosity beat his conscience. He tilted his head and leaned closer, trying to determine to whom she was speaking.

"Hello? Hello? Can you hear me? Hello?" Blaire spoke into her cellphone while standing on the edge of her bed. Her back faced away from the door. "Hello? Okay, now I can hear you. I have to say, I'll never complain about cell phone service back home. There is about a two-inch area of space I get reception in this town, and it happens to be on top of my bed while standing on one foot."

After a few seconds, Blaire continued, "Yeah, oh good, you got my email. I didn't know if I'd be able to get through with my phone, but I wanted to try. I need some advice, and I have news."

He should leave. He was violating Blaire's trust standing here. Regardless, Felipe's feet remained planted in place.

"I got an email from Dr. Sedgwick...I know, I couldn't believe it. I mean, I know he said he might consider, but still...it looks like a second chance—Mabel, Mabel, slow down. What are you talking about? Of course, I remember how they treated me, but finishing fellowship...well, you know that's been my dream since...well, you know."

After a minute of silence, Blaire responded, "Plus, there are my parents. Can you imagine if I stayed here? Can you picture that? It's crazy, right? No, I have to come home. I have to get back to reality."

Felipe couldn't hear the rest of Blaire's debate, but he didn't need to listen to it. He stepped away from the door and shook his head. He hurried to his door, opened and closed it behind him quietly, and leaned his back against it, sliding to the ground.

Clenching his fists, Felipe rested his head against the door and stared at the ceiling. What would life resemble once Blaire left? He didn't dare ponder the ramifications for his heart... *Back to reality.* He thought this was reality--at least for him. For him, his feelings for Blaire were real.

~

The next day, Blaire opened her eyes and stared overhead at a crack in the ceiling. It followed a serpiginous path and provided hours of distraction when needed in place of reliable cell phone service or television.

She'd spoken with Mabel the night before for over half an hour but still felt unsure about her decision to return home. Her final words to Mabel rung in her ears, "But I love him. I wish I didn't...it would be easier...but I love him."

Mabel had encouraged her and prayed for her guidance before saying goodnight.

Blaire pulled her gaze away from the crack, finding no answers there. She sat up in bed, stretched, and got ready for the day. Thirty minutes later, Blaire went downstairs, after inhaling a pre-packaged granola bar she'd brought with her on the trip. Standing at the front of the clinic near Juanita's empty desk, Blaire snuck a small bottle of sanitizer out of her blue scrub pocket. The isopropyl alcohol stung her nose and jolted her awake.

Blaire scanned the waiting room. A few patients trickled in and took their seats in the plastic chairs along the wall, waiting for Juanita to call each name. Blaire peered at her watch. *8:00 a.m. Where was Juanita?*

Felipe strode into the clinic's central hub with a stack of papers and a clipboard in his hand, wearing blue scrubs as well. His head stayed down, reviewing the sheets before him. When he lifted it, and his eye's landed on Blaire, his expression shifted. A grim frown formed on his lips, and several days-worth of stubble speckled his face. Dark circles hung below his eyes, and his furrowed brow deepened.

Blaire started to smile, but paused, realizing something had shifted. She lifted her hand and sent him a tentative wave. "Hey."

"What's wrong with you? You look exhausted."

He turned his attention back to his paperwork. "Where's Juanita?" He avoided her eye line.

Blaire stared at him, trying to sort out what had changed. "I don't know. I assumed you knew. She's usually here by now."

"I'm sure she'll be here soon. She's probably running late."

Flicking her eyes to the door to see if Juanita had arrived, her shoulder's tensed. "Yeah, I'm sure you're right. You know her better than I do… it's just...she's usually the first one here."

"I'm sure she'll be along soon." Felipe handed Blaire one of the sheets of paper without looking at her. "Here, why don't you get started with the first patient. We've got a full day, and since Juanita's not here yet to check people in and help with vitals, you'll have to get started on your own. I'll take the next guy and do intake and let you know when he's ready."

Blaire reached out and placed a hand on Felipe's shoulder.

Felipe snapped his head up, and his eyes clouded with anger. "What? We've got a lot of work to do today, especially since your time here is short." He took a step away from her and shifted his weight.

Dropping her hand, she searched his eyes. Finding no tenderness in them, her mouth settled into a tight line. "Right…right. Of course." She wanted to demand he tell her why he was upset. She wanted to fix things, but he was right. The patients continued to pile through the door, and there was a long day ahead. Tears filled her eyes, so she turned them to the paper Felipe gave her, focusing on it. "I'll take this guy back and get started—"

Juanita's next-door neighbor burst through the clinic front door. He wore a brown flannel shirt half-way tucked into his jeans and beads of perspiration puddled across his forehead. His cheeks flushed from exertion, and he gasped while clutching his chest. "Help! Someone has to help me!"

Felipe rushed over, Blaire right behind him.

She pulled her stethoscope off her neck, ready to begin her assessment. "Sir calm down and take a slow breath. Where does it hurt?"

He shook his head vigorously and gulped in air. "No---Not me. It's not for me. It' s—It's Juanita---she—"

Blaire squeezed the man's shoulder, giving him a shake. "She what? What's wrong with Juanita?"

The man let a small sob slip out amid his panting before he answered, "She collapsed. She's on the floor—at her house. We need help. Her husband's there, but he didn't know what to do."

The man didn't get another word out because Blaire rushed past him, almost shoving him aside. *No. It can't be true.* She couldn't let Juanita die. Juanita had become a close friend…almost a maternal figure in her life.

Memories flooded through Blaire's mind from the day Blaire

received the news from her parents that Megan had passed. Blaire had been in eighth-grade science class, and all she could think was that she should have been there. She hadn't been good enough to save her sister then, but she wasn't going to let Juanita die without a fight.

Hearing Felipe's steady footsteps behind her gave her courage. She didn't know why he'd acted distant with her today, but Blaire needed to set those thoughts aside and focus on saving her friend. The minutes that had passed since hearing the cry for help from Juanita's neighbor felt like hours. As she arrived at Juanita's house, the door stood open. As Blaire entered the doorway, her eyes landed on Juanita's body, still and lifeless on the floor. Juanita wore scrubs, and her bag lay next to her on the floor.

Juanita's husband stood rooted next to her, his face ashen and stunned. He didn't acknowledge Blaire and Felipe as they entered, other than to babble, "I—I—I didn't know what to do."

Blaire dropped to the floor next to her patient and placed her first two fingers at Juanita's neck. No pulse. Leaning closer to Juanita's mouth, Blaire looking and listening for breath sounds. None.

Blaire shook her head at Felipe. "She's not breathing, and there's no pulse. Start CPR."

Felipe began a round of chest compressions, and Blaire gave two rescue breaths.

She didn't question the sanitary ramifications, but rather Blaire had only one thought--save Juanita.

They continued with this cycle for two minutes before Blaire lifted her hand, indicating for Felipe to pause.

She rechecked Juanita's pulse. Nothing. Still nothing. Blaire flicked her eyes to Felipe. He looked like a scared little boy--hoping for a miracle, too broken and naïve to accept anything less.

He pleaded with his eyes. "We have to save her. We can't give up. Let's go again." He began compressions once more, placing one hand on top of the other on the breastbone. He interlocked his fingers so tightly they turned white.

Blaire readied herself, preparing to breathe for Juanita again. They couldn't call for an ambulance--the hospital was too far away, and Juanita would never make it. A thought came to mind. "Felipe, does the clinic have an AED? We haven't had to use it...so I didn't know...but does it?" She leaned over and gave her two breaths before he resumed his part of the cycle.

"We have one. It's in the second exam room under the sink in the cabinet. It's in a yellow case. There's a small crash kit next to it, too."

She raised her head and caught Juanita's husband's gaze. "Sir."

He didn't look at her. He didn't move at all.

Blaire looked up again at the husband. "Sir, I need you to run to the clinic and bring back the AED. It's a defibrillator. We need it to help your wife. And there should be a small bag next to it. Bring that, too."

The man's head snapped to attention, and he took off like a dart. Within minutes he returned with the AED and kit in tow.

Blaire opened the yellow case and placed the pads on Juanita's chest. She turned on the machine, waiting for it to read the patient's rhythm. The device told them to clear the patient and prepare to administer a shock. Blaire whipped her eyes to Felipe.

He gave Blaire a small nod.

"Clear," she shouted before pressing the shock button.

Juanita's chest arched, and her body shook in sync with the jolt of electricity from the machine.

Blaire waited for a moment to see if the AED picked up a response from the patient. She placed her fingers on Juanita's neck again. Still, no pulse.

Felipe resumed compressions, and the two of them carried on for at least thirty more minutes.

Blaire rested her hand on top of Felipe's, which perched above Juanita's chest, ready to begin compressions again. "Felipe."

He didn't meet her eyes.

She grabbed both of his hands in hers. "Felipe—I—I think she's gone. I think we have to call it."

He shook his head, and tears filled his eyes. "No. No, she can't be gone."

Tears pooled behind Blaire's eyes, and her throat tightened. It became hard to swallow, but she gulped down her grief and tried to find the right words, "I—I'm sorry. I'm so, so sorry."

He lifted his head, and his eyes flashed with anger. "You're sorry? You're sorry? For what exactly? It's not like Juanita meant anything to you. It's not like this town, or the clinic means anything to you. So, how can you be sorry? You're a volunteer, passing through. You don't deserve to be sorry. You don't get that right."

Placing a hand to her chest, Blaire flinched. "What do you mean? Of course, this place matters to me…Juanita matters to me…you matter to me."

Felipe snorted and clenched his jaw. Refusing to meet her gaze, he growled, "Yeah, right. I know you're leaving to get back to your real life. If you're going to leave, then why don't you just leave. No point in dragging it out."

"I—I, don't know what you're talking about," she stammered, "I—I." Blaire jumped up and turned to Juanita's husband, who huddled in the corner of the room sobbing. "Sir, I'm sorry for your loss. We did everything we could to help her. She was a wonderful person. I—I'm sorry." With her final apology, she fled the house and ran down the road.

Blaire didn't know where to go, not knowing the area well. She couldn't face the familiar people in the clinic, waiting to hear what happened to their dear friend and nurse, Juanita.

Pumping her legs, Blaire ran away from yet another disappointment, another failure she'd delivered to important people in her life. As she raced down the road, dark clouds filled the sky. Large, heavy droplets of water fell from above and mingled with the tears pouring down her face.

Her hair became wet and stuck to her neck and cheeks. She couldn't breathe. She wanted the rain to wash away all of it--the pain in Felipe's eyes, the death of her newfound friend, and her fear of letting everyone down. If it could remove all the germs, all the bad things in life, maybe she'd feel clean and whole. Maybe she could breathe again.

After jogging for at least a mile or two, Blaire stopped and stared at the muddy road before her. Home. She'd thought Santiago del Alma could become her home, but she'd been wrong. It was time to go home and face the life she'd left behind, including all of its messes. She'd lost everything; love, friendship, and a future she'd dare to imagine for herself.

Now, all Blaire wanted was to get as far away from Guatemala and heartbreak as possible. She turned on her heel and began a slow jog back to the clinic. When she got to her room, she'd call the airline and be on the first plane home.

Chapter 26

"You Can't Go Home Again"

Blaire burst through the clinic's front door, wearing soaking wet and mud-caked scrubs. Her hair matted to her cheeks from sweat and precipitation, and her tennis shoes sloshed with each step.

Blaire thought she must look horrific. She spoke to the crowd, but her voice sounded detached and foreign, "I'm sorry... there's been an emergency. You'll all have to reschedule your appointments. I apologize for the inconvenience."

Many people huddled around, asking Blaire if she was okay and what had happened.

Instead of answering them, she walked toward the stairwell leading to her bedroom.

As she left the room, the patients trickled out the front door, and Blaire wondered if she should lock it, but decided there was no point. The worst had already occurred.

She opened the door to her bedroom, grabbed her phone, and punched in the airline's number.

A southern drawl answered the line, "Hello, this is RightWay Airlines, how may I help you?"

"Yes, this is Blaire Cunningham. I'd like to book a one-way ticket to La Guardia Airport."

"No problem, ma'am, I need your date of birth, credit card information, and the date you wish to travel."

Blaire dispensed the information through wracking sobs. She covered her mouth in between phrases, hoping she didn't sound like a crazy woman. "I—want—to—leave—here—as—soon—as—possible."

The voice sounded concerned, "Ma'am, are you okay?"

"I'm—okay." She was not okay.

After a few seconds, the woman rattled off flights leaving Guatemala City over the next two days.

The gasping and crying had subsided a bit, and Blaire sucked in a long breath before speaking again. "I'll take the one tomorrow night, please. The one at 7:00 p.m."

"Okay, ma'am, I've got you all set, and I'm sendin' a confirmation email in case you need to reschedule. Any trips booked have a no change fee for the first twenty-four hours."

"Trust me, I won't change my mind. I don't belong here…I don't belong anywhere, but definitely not here. Not anymore."

"So, you're heading home?"

"I don't have a home," Blaire whispered, hanging up the phone and placing it on her nightstand.

She stared at the empty hallway beyond her open bedroom door, willing Felipe to appear and tell her everything had been a mistake. He'd say he loved her and didn't want her to leave. Then, he'd inform her that Juanita was fine, and the past few hours had been a bad dream.

She scanned the room, taking in the space that initially appeared dark, dingy, and off-putting but had come to provide comfort and acceptance. Blaire had started to think of the clinic and this town as home. How strange that in another day she'd be sitting in a New York City airport, rejoining her place in the bustling city she'd fled for adventure and answers. Had she found any?

She still had to face her fellowship director and make a decision about her career. Her germaphobia had improved, although not wholly abated. Her love life was abysmal; that couldn't be argued. Then there was Stella Cunningham. Looming on the horizon was Megan's Gala and Blaire's responsibility to attend as the diligent Cunningham and younger sister to the deceased. Not that she didn't want to honor Megan's memory—she did. She just didn't want to deal with her parent's world and their expectations.

Blaire sniffled and wiped away the remaining moisture on her cheeks with her fingers. She dried her hands on her scrubs. These were the clothes she'd worn when Juanita passed--the realization nearly knocked Blaire over. She gasped for air. Wrenching the edges of the top, Blaire struggled to get the clingy shirt off, as if it were responsible for the horrors of the day. If she could remove it, maybe she could breathe.

Flinging it aside, Blaire replaced her wet clothes with a clean set of pajamas. She lifted the top sheet off her bed, ready to slide underneath it and put an end to the day, but her eyes fell upon her phone on the nightstand.

Picking it up, she stood on her bed--the one area she could reliably get cellular service. Standing on her tiptoes, she punched Tiffany's numbers into her phone. She listened to the ringing, letting her mind wander to the day's earlier events. *Juanita was dead. And so was a relationship with Felipe.*

Tiffany's warm voice broke Blaire's reverie, "Hello?"

"Tif-Tiffany?"

"Blaire? Are you okay? What's going on?" her voice resonated with concern.

Blaire scrunched her eyes closed tight and shook her head,

though Tiffany couldn't see her. "N-No. Not really. Something terrible happened, and I'm coming home tomorrow. Can you pick me up at the airport? And would it be okay if I stayed with you for a little while longer?"

"Sure, sure. Of course. Do you want to talk about what happened?"

Blaire let a long, shuddering sigh slip out of her lips. "Well, the short story is that Felipe and I broke up, and I'm coming home so I can rectify the travesty that my life has become. I need to message my program director and set up a meeting, so I don't blow that, too."

"Oh, Blaire, I'm so sorry about you and Felipe. Are you sure things are over? Maybe you two can work things out?" her voice lilted up at the end of her question, carrying a hopeful tone.

"I don't think so, Tiff. I'd say it's over. Like over, over. We lost a patient today, and he's angry with me. Plus, I'm sure he's disappointed that I'm leaving him in the lurch. His clinic will have to close. Anyways, I can't think about this stuff right now. Also, I have to get home for Megan's Gala. I'm not excited about seeing my mother, but I owe it to Megan to make the Gala a success. It's the least I can do now. It's the only thing I can do now."

Tiffany sighed. "Okay. Well, I'll be there to pick you up. I'll see if Mabel can ride with me or meet us at my apartment afterward, and then we can get a full report from you about the trip."

"Thanks. I'll see you tomorrow. I'll text you the details of the flight as soon as I hang up, although you might not get the text right away. It's the flight out tomorrow at 7:00 p.m. If you don't get my text. I'm flying into La Guardia. Love you, Tiff."

"Love you, too. See you tomorrow." The line went dead as Tiffany hung up the phone.

Blaire sat the phone on the nightstand and slid underneath her sheets. She leaned over and dimmed her nightstand lamp, settling her head on the pillow. Closing her eyes, she prayed, "God, I don't know what I'm doing. I don't know if I'll ever be good enough…for anyone. I let everyone down—Juanita, Felipe, my parents, Megan, even myself. Help me, Lord. I don't know what to do, but I can't stay here."

She fell into a welcome sleep, but not before having a final thought that she hadn't used any hand sanitizer for the past few hours.

~

Blaire woke up the next day and briefly forgot the horrible events that had transpired the day before. She peeked out her door to ensure Felipe was not in sight, before dashing to the shower and returning to her room to get dressed.

The scrubs she'd worn the day before sat crumpled in a damp pile on the floor. She picked them up, rushed to the bathroom, and shoved them into the metal trash can. Blaire pressed the scrubs down with her fists, trying to push away the terrible memories they carried with them.

A sob threatened to erupt, but she tamped it down. Scurrying back to her bedroom, Blaire folded her remaining clothes into neat piles and placed them in neat stacks in her suitcase. Once all her things were packed, she zipped the suitcase shut and rested her hand on top.

Blaire hung her head but willed herself to press forward. She needed to run to the clinic's exam rooms and make sure she hadn't forgotten anything.

Jutting her head out her doorway, Blaire looked both ways. With the hallway clear, she jogged downstairs. A glance at her phone confirmed the time: 8:00 a.m. The clinic remained closed today in honor of Juanita.

Blaire imagined Juanita's husband would be making arrangements today for a funeral or memorial service. She hated she would miss it. Retrieving a small medical bag from one of the exam rooms, tears threatened to spill over, and her throat tightened as she surveyed the empty space.

She'd never have imagined a few weeks ago that she'd come to think of this place as home. Blaire hurried to her room, called the next-door neighbor, and asked if he could take her to the airport. She'd be a million hours early for her flight, but she didn't care. Blaire couldn't stay here and chance running into Felipe. She rubbed her arm, hugging herself tight.

Grabbing two suitcases and her purse, Blaire dragged the oversize bags behind her. She'd decided to purge as much as possible, leaving behind her extra freeze-dried food, soap, and hand sanitizer. This freed up two bags that she left for the clinic to use or toss away if they saw fit.

As she struggled down the stairs, Blaire grunted. Arriving at the bottom stair, she stopped and wiped away beads of perspiration from her forehead. The summer humidity hung heavy in the air despite it still being early morning. She leaned down, ready to grasp the handles of her suitcases again when she heard someone clear their throat. Blaire released the handles and stood upright.

In front of her stood Felipe wearing a green short sleeve shirt with dark blue jeans. He ran a hand through his hair, and it fell across one brow. His deep brown eyes gazed at her intently, and he frowned. "Leaving now?"

Blaire shrugged and gave him a small nod. "Yeah, I am…listen…I—I." She searched for the right words, shifting her eyes to the floor. She lifted her head again and shifted her weight. "I have to go."

At that moment, the next-door neighbor came through the clinic front door. "Señorita? Ready to go?"

She stared at Felipe. *Say something. Please…say something.*

His lips remained closed, and he clenched his jaw.

Blaire whispered, "Goodbye," and grabbed her bags, pulling them behind her. She looked toward the neighbor. "I'm ready to go."

Those were the last words Blaire spoke to Felipe, and she

imagined it would be the last time she'd see him or the town she'd grown to love. Pausing at the neighbor's truck, Blaire let the man put her luggage in the truck bed.

She took her place in the passenger seat and pondered what came next. Reaching into her bag, she pulled out a container of hand sanitizer and squirted it into her hand. As she rubbed it in, Blaire marveled that it didn't provide the comfort to her she'd once felt. She didn't feel clean or safe. At last, a torrent of tears spilled, and this time she didn't hold them back.

Chapter 27

"Love Conquers All?"

Felipe watched Blaire walk out the front door toward his neighbor's truck. He spun around and took quick strides to his office, flicking on the dim light as he entered it. Sitting down at the desk, he flipped his laptop open, hoping to find a distraction or answer to one of his mounting problems.

While the server logged him into his email, he closed his eyes and filled his lungs with air. *Juanita was gone. Everyone he loved left him.* Felipe spoke aloud to the silence surrounding him, "What did I do wrong here, God. I've lost my family, the clinic, and now Juanita. She was like a second mother to me. And now, Blaire. She'll never forgive me for the way I acted and the things I said."

He opened his eyes, and the first email in his inbox carried the subject line "fear and love."

It was probably junk mail, but something made him click on it.

Once he did, the email contained an advertisement for a free daily spiritual newsletter and a single verse. Today's verse said, "There is no fear in love."

There is no fear in love. God's truth pierced his heart. He didn't know how he would do it, but he was determined to win Blaire back and save the clinic. He wouldn't go down without a fight. He owed it to his community, himself, and God to not be afraid. He couldn't fear losing love--he needed to take a chance.

He jumped up from his desk and grabbed his phone. Heading upstairs to Blaire's empty room, he searched for a phone signal. After finding one bar, he dialed a friend.

"Hey Jose, it's Felipe. I need a favor. Can I borrow your truck?"

"Sure, Felipe, no problem, but I'm in the middle of something, and I can't get over there for a few hours."

"A few hours?" Felipe peered at his watch, noting the time, 11:00a.m. It took several hours on a good day to get to the airport, and that was if there was no traffic and perfect weather. "Okay, that's fine, but hurry. It's urgent."

Felipe hung up and tried to keep himself busy while he waited for his friend.

Jose did not arrive until 4:00 p.m. and found Felipe pacing outside the clinic. "Sorry, it took longer than I thought to finish up, but I'm here now."

Felipe ran to Jose's truck. "Thanks, Jose. I can't miss it."

Jose tossed the keys to Felipe and raised an eyebrow. "Miss what?"

Felipe slid into the driver's seat, slammed the door, and shoved the key in the ignition. Sticking his head out the open window, he ignored his friend's question. "Thanks, Jose! I'll get it back to you as soon as I can." With a wave of his hand, Felipe tore down the road. His hands trembled at the thought of declaring his feelings to Blaire. Glancing at the clock on the truck dashboard told him time was running out--he hoped he wasn't too late.

~

The truck pulled into the parking lot in front of the airport at 6:13 p.m. *Two minutes.* In two minutes, Blaire would board the only flight scheduled to depart Guatemala and land in New York City tonight.

Felipe jumped out of Jose's truck and slammed the door. Running to the airport's front door, he prayed under his breath, "Please let her still be here. Please." Dodging people milling about the front of the airport, Felipe weaved through the line forming at the check-in desk.

A middle-aged woman standing in the queue with her teenage son planted her hands on her hips. "Hey, you cannot jump in front of people like that."

Felipe usually would wait his turn--polite and obedient. Not today. He tossed a wave over his shoulder and gave a desperate apology, "I'm sorry, it's an emergency. I can't wait today."

He shoved his way to the front of the line, apologizing along the way. Placing both hands on the counter, Felipe caught his breath. He signaled to the airline clerk staffing the desk. "Sir. Sir, Stop the plane."

The man held a black phone handset to one ear and jotted notes on a paper while talking. He paused his conversation, balancing the phone between his shoulder and his ear. He shifted his eyes to the source of his interruption. "May I help you?"

Still breathing heavily after jogging from the parking lot, Felipe spoke between labored breaths, "I said, I—need—you—to—stop—an—airplane. Please."

The man's jaw dropped, and he gave Felipe a quizzical frown before bursting into laughter. "Ah, you're kidding. It's a joke. Haha, sir. Very funny. Who put you up to this? Was it Victor?"

Felipe shook his head. He'd finally regained his breath. "No. I'm not joking. I'm serious. There's a woman on an airplane, and I'm in love with her. I can't let her leave. If she leaves, things might never be the same. It might be too late. I don't think she'll come back. Please."

The clerk's eyes softened, and he sent Felipe an understanding smile. "Sir, I sympathize with you, I do. However, I don't have the authority to ground an airplane. I'm sorry."

An idea formed in Felipe's mind, and he raised his brow. "Hey, could you get me on the flight that's headed to New York City at 7:00 p.m.?"

The attendant typed a series of letters and numbers into the computer screen before him and then shook his head. "I'm sorry, sir, but that flight has already boarded. They locked the gate one minute ago, and there are strict laws against reopening it. I'm afraid there's no way to get you on that plane. Would you like me to get you on the next flight to New York?"

Felipe debated. He could return home and try to find a new purpose for his life, now void of the one person with whom he'd want to spend his future, or he could face his fear and take a chance. *No fear.* "Okay, yeah, that'd be great. When is the next flight?"

The man clicked away again on his keyboard with his gaze focused on the small computer screen. He scanned the list and flicked his eyes back to Felipe. "Unfortunately, there's a terrible storm that is supposed to be coming through tonight and through tomorrow. It looks like the rest of the flights out tonight are delayed or canceled. The earliest I can get you out of here is two days from now." He raised his eyebrows. "Will that work?"

Felipe ran his hand through his hair and sighed. "Yeah, I guess it'll have to work. Thanks. Book it."

The gentleman made a few more taps on the keyboard and a rectangular white and black ticket printed out from a machine below. He handed the ticket to Felipe and grinned. "I hope you get the girl. She must be special to go through all this trouble."

Nodding his head, Felipe grinned. "Yeah, she is special. In fact, I don't think I've ever met anyone else like her." He took the ticket from the clerk. "Thanks," Felipe uttered before turning around and weaving his way through the off-put crowd he'd line-cut, tossing, "sorry and excuse me," as he went.

He hurried to his borrowed truck and slid in, his hands shaking as he turned the key in the ignition. Placing both hands on the steering wheel, Felipe dropped his head and said a quick prayer for the next forty-eight hours. In forty-eight hours, he'd have his answer. He put the truck into gear and pulled away, driving toward his future.

~

Blaire exited her airplane, thankful to have two feet on the ground again. Even though she'd made progress, she couldn't resist the urge to pull out her hand sanitizer and give herself a spruce of gel.

She headed to the baggage claim and collected her two large suitcases off the carousel. Lugging them behind, she walked to the passenger pick-up area. She stood waiting, trying to find Tiffany's car in the sea of vehicles at the curb.

A voice interrupted her search, "No way. No way that is our Blaire. Not in those shoes. And carrying only two suitcases? And where's the disinfectant spray at the ready?" Mabel stood a few feet away wearing a black pencil skirt and blazer, heels, and a smirk.

Tiffany rushed toward Blaire and threw her arms around Blaire's neck. "Aah! We missed you so much! I can't believe you're home. You're really, really home. And in one piece."

Mabel squinted her eyes, examining her friend. "You look different. Good different, but different."

Blaire smiled. "I feel different. Not good yet, but Guatemala definitely changed me."

Waving the other two to follow her, Mabel tilted her head toward the white four-door car waiting for them. "Well, come on. Let's head to Tiffany's, and you can fill us in along the way on all these changes."

Blaire grabbed one bag, and Tiffany took the other one. She followed her two friends and slipped into the car, trying to find the words to describe the past few weeks. *Had it really only been a few weeks?*

She drove along with her two best friends and rode in silence other than giving them short one or two-word answers to specific questions.

Once they arrived at Tiffany's apartment, the three girls carried Blaire's luggage upstairs and unloaded them into Tiffany's spare bedroom. The room was tidy, and in Blaire's absence, it appeared Tiffany had stowed all of her things. "It looks like you cleaned up around here."

Tiffany smiled and nodded. "Yeah, I've got all of your stuff organized, don't worry. Everything is in boxes under the bed or in the closet."

"Thanks for keeping everything for me."

"Okay, so we didn't press you too much on the way over here," Mabel sent a stern, pointed stare to Blaire, "but now's the time. Spill."

Wracking sobs overtook Blaire. She sank onto the edge of the guest bed, crying and rocking herself back and forth.

Mabel and Tiffany flanked her sides. Tiffany placed a hand against Blaire's head and urged Blaire to rest her head on her friend's shoulder. "It's okay. You can tell us...you don't have to be perfect."

"I messed up. I messed up in a big way. I got in a fight with Felipe...I don't even know what it was about, really. I think it was because neither of us wanted me to leave, but that's not what we said. Then, a good friend passed away. She had a heart attack, and Felipe and I did CPR, but she didn't make it. She was like a second mother to him. He's lost so much, and I couldn't save her."

Mabel took one hand and placed it delicately on Blaire's shoulder and gave her a few stiff pats. "It's okay. It's going to be okay."

Blaire didn't know if it was the ridiculous state of her life or the out of character display of affection from Mabel, but she gave a small giggle. The giggles got away from Blaire, and before she knew it, all three girls were laughing hysterically. "It's inappropriate and makes no sense, but something about you patting me like that…it struck me as funny."

"I'm glad I can provide some comic relief for you," Mabel wiped away a tear and sent her friend another smirk.

"Thank you. I needed that, so thank you." Blaire rolled her shoulders back and cracked her neck. "Okay, what am I going to do, ladies? I'm supposed to meet my program director tomorrow. Oh, and I guess I'll need to see my mother, too, or at least talk with her because the gala is in two days. I don't have a lot of time. What am I going to do? Do I just try to forget Felipe and everything that happened?"

Tiffany squeezed Blaire's shoulder. "I don't think you forget that it happened. I think you take tonight and pray about it… you'll know what to do in the morning. You need some rest. Why don't you shower and change clothes? I believe your clothing boxes are in the front of the closet if you need extra things. Do you want me to fix you something to eat?"

Lifting her head, Blaire turned to her friend and smiled. "No, thanks. I'm good. Thank you both for being here for me. I have the best friends."

Tiffany and Mabel left the room, and Blaire hopped in the shower. The warm water soothed her soul. She focused on the water, hoping it would wash away the sadness of the past few days. She stepped out of the shower and wrapped a towel around her body. Thinking about her clothes in her suitcases, Blaire couldn't bear to open the case and see the things she'd worn in a place that had caused so much joy and pain.

She opened her friend's closet, and her eyes fell upon a brown box labeled with large, black letters saying, "Blaire's clothes."

Blaire opened the lid and was pleased to find a set of black and white pajamas. She removed them from the box, and a small book tucked inside them fell to the floor. Her eyes landed on it, and she recognized it at once. The cover was red, worn leather, and shiny, gold letters embossed in the center read, "Holy Bible." It was Megan's Bible. She'd seen her sister read from it many times. Often, her sister scribbled notes in it with different colored pens.

Blaire's hand quivered as she leaned down to pick it up, her body still encased in her towel. The room's air conditioning chilled her bare shoulders but didn't care. Blaire hadn't seen Megan's Bible in years. It must have been shoved in the back of a drawer and forgotten. The first few years after Megan's death, Blaire had wanted nothing to do with the book. Reading Megan's thoughts sounded too painful. But now...now something made Blaire pick up the book and open it.

She sank down on the edge of the bed and opened the front cover. The first page displayed her sister's name, Megan Cunningham, in their grandmother's shaky cursive, as the Bible had been a gift for her sister's tenth birthday. Blaire's grandmother had been the sole Cunningham besides Megan with compassion and tenderness. Blaire suspected she was the person who led Megan to a relationship with God.

Flipping through the first few pages, Blaire fingered the onion-skin paper, noting its smooth texture. She lifted the book closer to her face and inhaled. It still smelled like a mixture of her grandmother's floral perfume and Megan's citrus shampoo. Blaire's throat tightened. She could close the book and put it away. Pretend it didn't exist. Leave things alone and go back to fellowship, hand sanitizers, and unrelenting perfectionism.

Blaire shook her head, resolute. No. She was not going backward. Pressing her left thumb between the middle of the book, she opened it and flipped through several pages before one caught her eye and gave her pause. It held Megan's loopy handwriting in bright pink ink pen in the margin. She closed her eyes for a second, imaging the healthy, teenage version of her sister writing her precious, innermost thoughts.

When Blaire opened her eyes, she drew in a deep breath and started reading. There was a verse underlined three times half-way in the middle of the page; 1 John 4:18-19. "There is no fear in love. But perfect love drives out fear because fear has to do with punishment. The one who fears is not made perfect in love. We love because He first loved us."

The word perfect and punishment pierced Blaire's heart. It was as if she were reading about her childhood—a life filled with impossible expectations and withholding of praise and love as a result.

Blaire's eyes filled with tears, and she wiped the first set away. She cast her gaze to the margin where her sister had written, "Perfect love! God gives me His perfect love because he loves me. Not for anything I did or deserve, but because of who He is—God. If I have His perfect love, there's nothing to fear. I can do ALL things through Christ who strengthens me."

The room remained empty, but Blaire spoke aloud, "I thought it was me. I thought I wasn't good enough. Megan, you always seemed good enough, perfect, really, even though I knew you weren't. But mother and father saw you that way. And I couldn't measure up to the bar you set. It's not your fault, but it's not my fault either, I guess. Perfect love getting rid of all my fears. That sounds…freeing."

Blaire bowed her head and whispered a short prayer, "God, I don't want to be afraid anymore. I don't want to wipe down all the surfaces and relationships in my life, afraid to get messy. I want to live the way you want me to live—without fear and walking in Your love. Please help me to do it."

Goosebumps prickled at Blaire's arms, and she shivered. Tears now flowed down her cheeks, but a smile tugged at the corners of her lips. Free. She finally felt free. Blaire rose and put on her clean pajamas. She stared at the damp towel she'd tossed to the ground and thought she could just leave it there. She was free now...but it wouldn't do anyone any good if mildew and mold ruined a good towel, would it? She stared at it again and decided to pick it up and fold it, not because she wasn't free, but because there was no reason to become a total slob in this new life season.

She chuckled. Thinking a bold first step might be throwing away her mounds of sanitizer and wipes, Blaire marched to her suitcases. She yanked out all her degerming supplies and carried them into Tiffany's kitchen.

Tiffany and Mabel sat on the couch with their heads huddled close in an intense but whispered conversation. They both lifted their heads upon Blaire's entrance and stopped talking.

Mabel eyed the mountain of disinfectants in Blaire's arms and furrowed her brow. "Uh, what are you doing? I thought you were going to bed. What are you carrying—wait—are those all your sanitizing things?"

Blaire didn't pause to explain herself other than to quip a quick, "Yep," as she strode to the trash can, pressed her foot on the lever, and dumped all her precious supplies in the garbage.

Walking to her friends, she plopped on the couch and turned to face them. "Okay, ladies, I need your help. I've had a revelation."

Mabel rolled her eyes to the ceiling. "I'm afraid to ask."

Taking a softer approach, Tiffany reached over Mabel and placed a hand on Blaire's arm. "Blaire, honey, don't you think you need rest tonight? We can figure everything out in the morning. Things always look different in the morning light."

Blaire stared at Tiffany, determined to stress her commitment to this revelation. "Nope. We have to start tonight. There's no time."

Tilting her head, Mabel narrowed her eyes at her friend. "No time for what?"

"No time to waste. I have to send an email tonight to my Program Director and tell him thanks, but no thanks. I'm going to pass on the second-year fellowship position. Then, I need to figure out the best way to tell my parents I'm going to permanently live in Guatemala...and help run the clinic...with Felipe...if he'll have me and if it's not too late to save the clinic.

And I need a dress to wear to Megan's Gala and work up the courage to make a speech—"

Mabel cut her off, "Wait," she held up a hand, "you don't do public speaking. In all the years I've known you, the only time you've given a speech is to educate the two of us on the importance of hand hygiene and covering your cough. In fact, if I recall correctly, you once told me you gave a speech in high school and fainted."

Blaire nodded her head. "That's true. I did faint, but that was then, and this is now. I'm a new person. I'm going to cast out the fear because I have God's perfect love."

Both of her friends wore puzzled expressions and simultaneously said, "What?"

"It's something I read in the Bible. And it's true, and it's changed me. I'm a new woman." She spread her hands open. "See, I dumped out all my sanitizing stuff. Don't get me wrong, I'll still wash my hands, I'm not going to become gross or anything, but I'm done with the old, perfectionistic, germaphobic me. I'm ready to live my life without fear. I suppose working in the clinic provided some exposure therapy, but what I read in Megan's Bible drove the point home. So…"

Tiffany smiled. "So, what?"

"So, are you guys going to help me walk into my new life? We've got forty-eight hours." Blaire glanced at the clock on the wall in Tiffany's living room. "Actually, less than that, so if you two are going to help me pull this off, we need to start planning tonight." She looked at both of her best friends, hopeful.

Tiffany clapped her hands together.

Mabel sent her a wide grin, stood, and then said, "Well, don't just sit there. Let's do this."

Jumping off the couch, Blaire hugged her two friends, thankful she didn't have to face her fears alone.

~

The early morning sunlight crept through the partially closed blind in Tiffany's living room. The sliver of light caused Blaire to open one eye as she lay on Tiffany's couch with her face half-way buried into a pillow. Blaire pushed herself to a seated position and looked around the room. Mabel lay prone on the floor with a grey knit blanket flung across her curled body and an extra couch cushion underneath her head. Tiffany was nowhere in sight.

The aroma of fresh-brewed coffee intermixed with peppermint creating an odd, if not alerting, scent. Blaire turned her attention toward the source of the fragrance and saw Tiffany busy in the kitchen. "How long have you been up?" Blaire stretched her arms overhead and yawned.

Tiffany stood behind the kitchen counter, making coffee, toast, and hot tea. Ah—the source of the peppermint smell.

Blaire shook her head. She couldn't convert Tiffany to team coffee, but at least her friend didn't force her herbal concoctions on others.

Tiffany smiled. "Not too long. I know you have a busy day ahead, and I thought we should start the day with a good breakfast." She grabbed the two pieces of toast in the stainless-steel toaster and added them to a stack of bread on a white plate.

Blaire stood and walked into the kitchen, taking a seat at a barstool in front of the counter. Her stomach growled, and she plucked two slices of toast from the mountain of bread and a cup of steaming hot coffee from Tiffany. "What time did we go to bed last night? If you can call passing out on your furniture and floor going to bed."

Tiffany chuckled, helping herself to some tea and toast and taking a seat next to her friend. "I don't know for sure, but the last time I looked at my phone, it was after two a.m. I haven't stayed up that late since college."

Nodding her head, Blaire agreed, "Me neither, but we got a lot accomplished. I emailed Dr. Sedgewick, which, to be honest, I was dreading. I told him I appreciated everything he'd done for me, but I wouldn't be returning to the Infectious Disease Program and wished him the best. I tried to call Felipe to discuss things and let him know I would like to return to the clinic, but every time I called, the phone made a weird beeping sound."

Tiffany smacked her forehead. "I forgot to tell you last night, but I saw on my news app something about a brutal storm hitting Guatemala. Maybe he doesn't have cell service right now." She raised her brow.

Blaire shrugged. "I don't know. Maybe. I'll try again later today, but I can't think about that right now because the first thing on today's docket is facing Mr. and Mrs. Cunningham." She gave a half-smile to her friend. "Fun."

Mabel jutted her hand between the two girls sitting at the counter to reach for a piece of toast, startling Blaire. "Oh, don't let that Pharisee make you feel small. Remember, you are a child of God, and you may never be perfect enough for that mother of yours, but you are perfect in His eyes. You'll be fine. And if you're not, just call me, and I'll set her straight."

Blaire gulped down the remainder of her coffee and noted the green lights on the kitchen microwave. She gasped. "It's noon! We slept until noon. We have to go. I still need you guys to help me pick out a dress and shoes for the Gala tomorrow. I wrote that speech to plead for funds and more volunteers for the clinic, but it's a rough draft, and I'm terrible at public speaking, oh and I have to try to reach Felipe or the mayor—don't even get me started on that—what if I go to Guatemala and Felipe doesn't want me or the mayor already shut down the clinic, and I'm too late—oh, and I have to call my mother, and yes, I know, I know, big bad friend Mable will line her out, but honestly, Mabel I still have to explain things to her—she is my mother after all, and—"

Mabel put both hands in the air in surrender. "Woah, woah, woah. Take a breath. You have to calm down. You've got this. We're here to help you. As soon as you told us you were coming home, I took a few days off from the office. I'm at your service until after the Gala tomorrow night."

Exhaling a sigh, Blaire's torso relaxed. "Whew. Okay. Thanks, girls. I'm going to need your help, for sure."

Tiffany cleaned their dishes away and tossed napkins and crumbs in the trash. She turned to her worried friend and wore a teasing gleam in her eyes. "Hey, I was wondering if you had any hand sanitizer?"

"Tiffany, you know I threw all that stuff away last night. Just good old-fashioned hand washing at normal intervals for me. But if you really need some, there might—oh wait, you're kidding?"

Mabel and Tiffany erupted in a fit of giggles.

Blaire put her hands on her hips and frowned. "Haha. Glad you can laugh at my expense. Now come on, we can't afford to waste any more time."

The three friends tossed on their clothes, grabbed their bags, and shot out the door, ready to help Blaire conquer everything; her fears, hopes, dreams, and yes, even Stella Cunningham.

Chapter 28

"True Love Really Does Conquer All"

With flights delayed and canceled, Felipe couldn't get an earlier flight to New York City. The storm had also knocked out the local cell phone tower and internet, and service didn't resume until the day of his flight.

Since he couldn't leave sooner, and couldn't reach Blaire by phone or email, he did the next best thing—write.

He spent hours writing the exact words he wanted to say to her when he saw her. Then, he crumpled up the paper, tossed it in the trash, and started over--more than once. If Juanita had been here, she would have offered a word of wisdom to express himself and not be afraid of getting hurt.

He patted the final version of his letter, tucked securely inside his white dress shirt pocket. Picking up the handle on his rolling carry-on luggage, he saw Jose's truck approach. "Thanks, Jose, for the ride."

Jose waited for Felipe to take his seat in the cab next to him before taking off down the road. "Felipe, I thought you went to New York recently. Why are you headed back there so soon?"

Felipe's neck warmed, and he stared straight ahead. "I lost something... someone important, and I can't let her go. I'm going to go to make things right."

"Was it the pretty doctor who just left? Because I liked her, she seemed nice. A little funny about the wiping and cleaning everything, but nice."

"She was nice, Jose. To me, she was perfectly imperfect. And I love her...so I'm going after her."

Jose revved the engine and pressed down on the accelerator, forcing the truck along at a faster pace. "Well, then, let's make sure you make that flight on time." He went silent for a few minutes then spoke again, quieter this time, "I was sorry to hear about Juanita. I know how important she was to you."

Still staring ahead, Felipe tightened his jaw and fought back tears. "Thanks, Jose. She's part of the reason I'm going after Blaire. Juanita became my family after...after I lost mine, and I know she wanted me to find love someday and start my own family."

"Awe, that's beautiful, man," Jose teased.

Felipe punched him lightly on the shoulder. "Hey, you're just jealous I'm the one going after the gorgeous doctor."

Jose shrugged. "Can't argue with that, but seriously, I'm happy for you."

Felipe grinned. "Thanks."

The two men spoke little more the rest of the way to the airport, and as Felipe boarded his plane, all he could think about was Blaire's kind eyes and soft lips. He couldn't wait to wrap his arms around her and tell her the truth—he loved her and wanted to make a life with her. Felipe couldn't consider how he would feel if she said no. Instead, his focus was on the immense love bursting from his heart for Blaire Cunningham.

~

After hours of running from shop to shop trying on every dress and pair of shoes in New York City, Blaire, Tiffany, and Mabel returned to Tiffany's apartment and sunk onto the couch.

Mabel furrowed her brow. "You're going to have to call her. She's called you five times. As your friend, I can't let you get to number six. Come on, put on your brave face, and call your overbearing, unrelenting mother."

Blaire heaved a sigh and slapped her hands to her face, covering her eyes. "Ugh. Do I have to? Like do I really, really have to do it?"

Mabel pulled both hands off her friend's eyes and gave her a stern stare. "Yes, you have to. Now come on, what is it you doctors' always say? It's like pulling off a bandage. Just count to three and dial. It can't be as bad as you're imaging in your head."

Blaire sent her friend a deadpan expression, or at least she strove for whatever deadpan might look like. "Fine. Fine. I'll call my mother. But you don't fully appreciate the force that is Stella Cunningham."

Mabel guffawed. "Don't understand? Excuse me, but have you forgotten my grandmother? You don't have total dibs on troubled familial relationships." She shoved Blaire's phone in front of her friend's face. "Now, go on, call her."

Closing her eyes, Blaire said a silent prayer and then took the phone from her friend's hand. "Fine," she grumbled, pounding the numbers into the screen.

Her mother's voice answered on the third ring, "This is Stella Cunningham speaking."

"Uh—hi, I mean, hello, mother," Blaire uttered.

"Blaire, how many times have I told you not to mutter and stammer? I'm in a hurry, as you must know, because the gala is tonight. I need you to arrive early. Be there by 7:00 p.m., sharp. Not a minute late." Her mother ordered her about as if she might be one of the waitstaff.

"Mother—I'll be there, but the reason I'm calling right now is that I have something important to—"

Her mother cut her off, "Great, perfect, I'll see you tonight, and we can talk then. I have to go. You would not believe the idiocy I'm dealing with around here." Her mother started speaking to someone in the background, "Meredith, Meredith, how many times have I told you never to use carnations in the floral arrangements? Those will not work. Take them away." She jumped back to her conversation with Blaire, barked, "I'll see you tonight, Blaire, 7:00 p.m. Sharp," and hung up the phone.

Blaire stared at the blank screen. "Thanks, mother. Thanks for listening."

Tiffany walked over and rubbed Blaire's arm in support. "I guess you didn't get a chance to tell her about your plans to hijack the gala and plead for donations and volunteers for the clinic? Or that you're moving there as well?"

"No. Nope. I did not. Oh well, maybe it's for the best. My parents don't do bad news well, so maybe it's better if I spring it on them at the last possible minute."

Tiffany's forehead scrunched into a worried expression. "Maybe, but—"

"Never mind, we can't focus on my dysfunctional family right now. We have a gala to attend."

Mabel gave a nod and led the way to the bathroom to begin preparations. Two hours later, all three women wore stunning, floor-length ball gowns, high heeled shoes, and chignons that would put even Stella Cunningham to shame.

Blaire stared at her reflection in the mirror and turned her head side to side, admiring the French-twist Mabel had helped create. "Not bad. In fact, I'd say it's practically perfect." She sent Mabel a wink and glanced at the time on her phone. 6:15 p.m. "Well, if we want to grace my mother with our punctual presence, we better leave now. I checked the weather forecast earlier, and it's supposed to rain tonight, which means—"

Mabel cut her friend off, "Getting a taxi will be almost impossible. You're right, if we don't want to swim to the gala, we'd better head out now."

Blaire grabbed her bag and raced out Tiffany's front door with her two best friends following behind her. She hoped everything went well tonight. She prayed she still had a chance to save the clinic and her relationship with Felipe. It might be too late for both.

Arriving downstairs, underneath the apartment building's portico, Blaire noted the slight drizzle the weather channel called for earlier had turned into sheets of rain.

Mabel raised her arm in the air, hailing a cab. The taxi pulled up next to the curb and stopped, waiting for the three friends to enter.

Blaire held her black clutch over her head, trying to shield herself from the rain. She chastised herself for not remembering an umbrella.

The cab driver peered at them through the rearview mirror. "Where can I take you, ladies, this evening?"

Blaire glanced around the backseat of the cab and, for one second, thought about the germs it must harbor. Her grip tightened on her disinfectant-less clutch and replied, "The American Museum at Lincoln Center."

The man gave a small nod and pulled out aggressively into traffic, which moved at a snail's pace. The cab inched along a few feet at a time with horns blaring and people yelling from other vehicles around them.

Tiffany sat in between Mabel and Blaire and leaned forward to speak to the gentleman, "Um, sir, do you expect traffic to be like this all the way there? Even by New York standards, it seems like this is taking a lot longer than usual."

The man threw both hands in the air as the cab sat at a standstill again. "Who knows? It's been like this for the last two hours. It's the rain, and everyone is headed to Lincoln Center tonight. Must be some big event."

Blaire smiled, though the man couldn't see her. "Uh, I see. Well, I know you can't control the traffic, but if there are any secret side streets you know about or any long-time cab driver tricks to get around this mess, I'd be so grateful. We're headed to that big event tonight, and it's important we get there on time. Or early, actually."

The man gave a sarcastic chuckle. "Yeah, lady, I'll hop onto the sidewalk and take a super-secret shortcut right into the police station where they'll charge me with a moving violation and public endangerment."

Blaire frowned. "So, that's a no?"

Mabel looked at her friend as if Blaire had grown an extra head. "Uh, yes, that's a no."

With widened eyes, Blaire tossed her hands up. "What? It didn't hurt to ask. What are we going to do now? There's no way we will make it on time, and at this rate, we'll be doing well to get there before the whole thing ends."

Mabel glimpsed out her window. The rain fell in buckets, covering the window and windshield, so the world appeared blurry. She turned to Blaire. "We have to run for it."

Blaire's eyes widened further. "Run for it? Are you crazy? Did you get a good look out your window? We'll be soaked by the time we get to the gala. Beyond soaked."

Tiffany peeked at the time on her phone. 7:15 p.m. "Blaire. If we don't go now, I think we'll miss the entire gala. This car has barely moved since we got in it over half an hour ago. If we stay on the far side of the sidewalk under awnings, maybe we won't get drenched. Plus, if we leave right now, we should get there with a few minutes to get cleaned up before the gala starts."

Blaire considered her options. She could sit in this taxicab for the next several hours and disappoint not only her parents but also herself. There'd be no standing up to her parents, no pleading for support for the clinic, no chance at reclaiming the life Blaire wanted. Or she could jump out of the cab, run down the New York City sidewalk in a satin black ball gown and red-soled heels in a monsoon, and give it her best. It wasn't a perfect plan, but Blaire had learned that nothing in life was perfect. *Plus, it couldn't be worse than riding through the rain on a runaway horse.*

She turned to her friends and made the decision. "Okay, let's do it. Let's run for it." She tossed the cab driver an apology and enough money to cover the fare and a tip before sliding out her door, clutch overhead once again.

Blaire dashed down the sidewalk, weaving around people and running as fast as her stiletto-heeled feet would carry her. Once or twice, she glanced over her shoulder to ensure her friends were still alive.

Thankfully, much of the sidewalk leading to the American Museum remained under construction, which meant scaffolding provided intermittent protection from the rain. Still, in between the overhangs, the storm raged.

Blaire hadn't moved this fast since taking the physical fitness test in high school, and she experienced the same piercing side pangs she'd had back then. Clutching at her side, she chanted over and over, "I can do all things through Christ who strengthens me."

At one block out, Blaire heard Tiffany yell behind her. She stopped and turned around to see what had happened. "Are you okay?"

Tiffany nodded but winced. "Yeah, I think I sprained my ankle…and my heel broke." She bent down and picked up the offending footwear and the red pointed heel hinged open like a fish mouth.

"You're not getting anywhere on that thing." Blaire gave a defeated sigh.

Mabel stepped forward and caught Blaire's eye. "Go ahead without us. I'll take care of Tiffany. I'll get her to an urgent care and get her ankle evaluated. But you have a gala to attend. You've come too far to give up now."

Blaire flicked her eyes to Tiffany, hating to leave her injured friend behind.

Tiffany nodded and gave her a small smile. "It's fine, really. I'll be okay. Mabel will take care of me. You need to hurry. And I know you're trying to break free from the perfectionism and germaphobic thing, but a redo of your hair and a touch-up of makeup may be in order."

Tears of appreciation filled Blaire's eyes, and she chuckled. "I'm sure you're right. I hate to imagine what I look like right now. Are you sure?"

Tiffany bobbed her head. "I'm Sure. Go get your happily ever after."

A grin spread across Blaire's damp face. "Okay but call me as soon as you find out about that ankle." She spun around and pumped her legs, urging them and her heels not to fail her.

By the time she arrived at the American Museum entrance, the large clock on the bank's sign across the street read 7:55 p.m. Five minutes to spare.

Giving her name to the doorman, Blaire assured him she was on the list, despite her ragged appearance.

He waved her inside, and she scanned the room for the closest women's restroom. Finding it, she ducked inside and tried to repair the destruction caused to her dress, shoes, makeup, and hair by the rain. Blaire dabbed at her black dress with paper towels, thankful she'd worn a dark color at least. The rain splotches didn't show up too badly.

She wiped off her shoes and blotted her face before applying an extra layer of lipstick and blush. Her hair was the easiest save since she'd worn it up for the night. She smoothed it over the best she could with her hand and dried her arms and chest with more paper towels. Staring at her reflection in the mirror, Blaire determined she'd done the best given the circumstances. Definitely not perfect, but she guessed that was the point of the evening.

Surveying the room, Blaire both hoped to find her mother and father and prayed to avoid them at the same time. She wanted to tell them about her plans, but before she could locate her parents, a gala attendant approached her.

The young woman wore black dress pants, a white button-up shirt, and a headset. She spoke into the headset before turning her attention to Blaire. "Are you Blaire Cunningham by any chance?"

Blaire nodded and started to apologize, "I'm sorry I'm late. The weather was terrible, and I tried to take a cab, but then—"

The woman waved away Blaire's excuses. "No time for that now. Your mother nearly sent a search party out for you--she expected you here an hour ago."

Blaire glanced around the room once more, but still didn't see her mother anywhere. "That's right. Again, I apologize for the tardiness, but I need you to do something for me."

The woman raised a quizzical brow. "What's that?"

"I'd like to make a brief statement on stage, if possible. I want to share a few words…you know the gala is in my sister's memory, and…I have something I need to say."

The girl looked hesitant. "I don't know. I wasn't informed anyone other than your mother would be speaking tonight."

"Oh, well, I'm sure she won't mind too much. I am her daughter after all…and I'll keep it short, I promise." Stella Cunningham definitely would mind, but Blaire would deal with that fall out later.

"Well…I guess it would be okay. Maybe I should ask my supervisor—"

The young woman didn't get to finish her thought because Blaire took the brief acquiescence and plowed ahead, "Great, I'll go do that now, and I'll speak with my mother afterward."

Blaire scurried to the stage. Her palms began to sweat, and her throat tightened. She tried to gather her thoughts as she took the five stairs to the makeshift stage. She walked across it slowly and took her place behind a podium.

Blaire wrapped her right hand around the microphone, trying to steady herself. She prayed for God to calm her nerves--she hated public speaking. Opening her mouth to speak, nothing came out, so she cleared her throat. "Ahem."

The room grew still as everyone in the crowd turned their attention to the woman behind the podium.

Blaire gazed upon the hundreds of people and gulped. She could do this. "Um, excuse me. Hello. I wanted to say a few words. I'm Blaire Cunningham, Megan Cunningham's sister. Tonight is a special event held in honor of my sister's memory—a memory of a beautiful person whose warmth and generosity knew no bounds and whom I adored. Ever since I was a little girl, I wanted to grow up to be like her—she was perfect in my eyes. Megan made excellent grades, mastered athletics, was popular...but what I admired most was her determination to care for others—to give back.

She didn't get to do all the things she wanted to in life, but she did leave a lasting impression in my life, and I'm sure, in the lives of many others. Ever since she passed away, I've tried to make up for her absence. I've strived to be perfect like her. Recently I spent time in a community of people who taught me that I don't have to be perfect to do good or be enough. I'm enough already because God loves me. That's it. We're all made perfect in His love. And I know this may not make sense to all of you here tonight, but I wanted to share how Megan's love for the Lord inspired me to open my heart and mind to living life unafraid. So, I'm asking this entire room to open their hearts, and their minds, and yes, their pockets—"

Everyone in the crowd gave a chuckle.

"—to help save a clinic in rural Guatemala by giving donations of money or time. The clinic needs both. It needs more supplies, more medications, and more volunteers. It serves a lovely community of people who became like an extended family to me over the past month. In particular, one person touched my heart and taught me to love like Megan loved--freely. Thank you for your time, and please enjoy the rest of the evening. You can find me if you would like to support the clinic. Thank you."

The room erupted in applause, and warmth filled Blaire's cheeks. She hurried off the stage and made it to the bottom step when she heard a screeching voice.

"Blaire Elizabeth Cunningham. Have you absolutely lost your mind? To show up here looking like a wet dog and then take the stage dressed like that and say those things… you've, well, you've hijacked the event. What will people say?" Her mother stood before her with her hands planted on her hips, and her lips pressed together.

Blaire pulled in a long breath and let it out before responding, "Who are these people that we worry about what they will say? I'm sorry I was late, and I'm sorry I didn't get to talk to you beforehand, but I had to say those things. They were the right things to say. This evening is about Megan's memory, and I know she would be proud of me. I wanted to tell you yesterday, but you got off the phone so quickly that I couldn't—"

Her mother stepped closer. "Blaire, what are you saying? You are not making any sense."

"I'm not finishing my infectious disease fellowship. I'm heading back to Guatemala if the clinic will have me. I fell in love—both with a wonderful man and with the community. The clinic needs me, and I need it. I hope you understand, but even if you don't, even if you're disappointed in me, well, then, I'm okay with that. I still love you, but I have to live my life to please God and not others." Blaire spun on her heel and came face to face with Felipe Martinez.

He wore a black suit with a grey dress shirt with a black satin tie. His hair was slicked back, and Blaire had never seen him look more handsome.

Stepping forward, Felipe gave her a heart-melting grin. "Hi. Funny meeting you here."

She wanted to run into his arms, but she wasn't sure what his arrival meant. "What—what are you doing here?"

He walked closer, putting only inches between them. He took both her hands in his. "Same thing you are--fighting for the things I love. Blaire, I—I love you. I love you, and it scared me at first, but I want you in my life. I want you to come back to the clinic, work with me, and share a life with me. I love you. I tried to call, but there's been a storm, and I couldn't call out, and, oh, it doesn't matter—I don't want to be afraid anymore."

Tears filled Blaire's eyes, and she thought her heart might burst with happiness. "Neither do I. Did you hear my speech?" She raised her brow, hopeful.

He nodded and grinned. "I heard both your speeches. The one to your parents was more entertaining, though, I think you'll have to smooth things over with them in time. They are your parents, after all. But I liked the part about returning to a clinic and a person you loved. I'm hoping you were talking about me."

She smiled. "Of course, I was talking about you. I love you, Felipe. I love you. And yes, I'm coming back to Guatemala—if you and the clinic will have me and if we aren't too late to save it." She frowned.

Felipe cupped Blaire's face in his hand and stared into her eyes. "I don't think we're too late to save anything." He sunk down to one knee and clasped her hand in his. "Blaire Cunningham, you are the most fascinating, perplexing, infuriating, and wonderful woman I've met in my life. Will you marry me?"

Happy tears trailed down her cheeks, and she nodded. "Yes. A million times, yes."

He rose and reached inside his jacket pocket, pulling out a silver band. "I know it's not fancy, but this belonged to Juanita. Her husband wanted me to have it when I told him I was coming for you. He said having something she owned seal the hearts between two people she loved would have blessed her."

Now tears freely fell, and Blaire didn't attempt to stop them. "It's—it's perfect. Perfectly imperfect."

Felipe slipped the ring on her finger and tilted her chin toward his. He brushed his hand across her cheek, caressing it. Tracing his thumb across her jawline and he leaned in, pressing his lips against hers.

A shiver traveled down her spine, and her fingertips tingled. The kiss deepened, and she melted into Felipe's arms. All the worry from the past few days faded away, and she knew she was where God intended.

Felipe kissed her once more, then raised his head and placed his lips near her ear. He whispered, "I love you, Dr. Blaire Cunningham, and I always will."

She smiled and whispered back, "I love you, Felipe."

A band took the stage, and music filled the air. Felipe pulled his head back and gave her a grin. "May I have this dance?"

Blaire chuckled. "That depends…"

He raised an eyebrow. "On what?"

"Are you going to crush my pinky toe again?" She winked.

He laughed and lifted her hand, ready to move her around the room. "Well, I got your attention, didn't I? It may not have been the perfect plan, but it worked."

Blaire smiled and gazed at him. "It most certainly did."

Epilogue

"All's Well That Ends Well"

Almost two months later, Blaire stood in the middle of La Clinica almost and marveled at how a once foreign place now felt like home. She'd made some changes since her return—the once drab concrete walls were painted a bright blue color, and she'd hired a new nurse to work the front of the clinic. Also, the clinic hadn't wanted for volunteers or funding since her plea at Megan's Gala.

With added help around the clinic, she and Felipe could take extra trips to farms in outlying areas and provide care to even more patients than before.

Blaire had returned to Guatemala a few days after the gala with only two suitcases this time. Neither of them was filled to the brim with disinfectants.

Felipe raised his head as he finished with the last patient of the day. Placing his stethoscope around his neck, he sent her a smile and walked toward her. "Did you talk to your mom? When do we pick them up at the airport?"

That was the other good piece of news. Blaire's parents gained a newfound respect for their youngest daughter. She didn't know if she and her mother would agree on everything, or even most things. Still, they'd talked several times since the gala, and their relationship had improved with each conversation. The last time she spoke to her mother, Blaire had invited her to the wedding.

Blaire recalled her first day in Guatemala when Felipe picked her up at the airport in a chicken truck. She smirked.

Felipe lifted his brow. "What is that expression on your face about?"

Chuckling, Blaire shrugged. "Oh, nothing. I was thinking that my parents should have a complete rural experience."

"Blaire," Felipe warned, "We're not sending Jose in a chicken truck to pick them up, and if you and I arrive in one, I'm pretty sure your mother would faint."

Blaire cackled and then regained her composure. "I suppose you're right. Okay, no chicken truck. But can we at least take the dog with us?" She sent him a devilish grin.

"Listen, we're building bridges, Blaire. Hit the lights, and let's go. You've got a big day ahead, and, if I recall, Stella Cunningham does not like to be kept waiting."

Shaking her head, Blaire's soft, wavy hair bounced side to side. She turned off the last clinic light and followed Felipe out the door and into the beginning of her imperfect, messy, beautiful life. "No, no, she does not." She tacked a cream paper with silver embossed letters to the front of the clinic door.

Attention:
La Clinica will be closed tomorrow, September 30, for the
celebration of the joining of
Mr. Felipe Martinez
And

Dr. Blaire Cunningham
In Holy Matrimony
All Clinic Staff, Patients, and Community members are
welcome to attend the union at 2:00 pm at The Church
With a reception to follow

And they lived perfectly imperfectly ever after.

The End

About the Author

Jill writes inspirational romantic fiction with a medical theme. Her two debut novels are part of the *A Dose of Love* series. Each story can stand alone, but both feature strong female leads facing challenging life circumstances while finding love along the way. The third book in the series will release in the near future. Jill's debut novel, *Harte Broken*, was inspired by her love of romance and her walk through the grief of losing her mother on the same day of her daughter's birth. It raises the question, "What happens when the best day is also the worst one?"

Jill is a physician and mom, who loves coffee, travel, and anything glittered. She treasures spending time with her husband and children, who are her heart and greatest joy.